This book is from the imagination,
not history, but thoughts offered
a great soldier and Saint, with
admiration and love.

Judith Masefield

SHEPHERDESS

drawings by Leonard Weisgard

OF   FRANCE

remembrances of Jeanne d'Arc

by Judith Masefield

Coward-McCann   New York

Text © 1969 by Judith Masefield. Illustrations © 1969 by Leonard Weisgard. Published simultaneously in the Dominion of Canada by Longmans Canada Limited, Toronto. Library of Congress Catalog Number: 76-83488. Printed in the United States of America.

O God,
to whom I prayed
in the field
on the road
in battle
in the ruined chapel
the fort
the dungeon
and when the flames
were licking my poor body . . .
    take compassion
    on my beloved France.

am Jeanne the Shepherdess Soldier. I have descended to earth and would tell of my brief life. It ended before I was twenty years of age.

We were poor. One thing united us—our Faith. I was taught to follow the standard of virtue the Church held to be true. I believed that demons roamed abroad, enticing men to sin.

I have gone into the church of Domremy, where of old we heard Mass. Only the shell of it remains.

My home lay beside the church. It was here that I took my first Communion. I wore a little round cap on my unruly hair. A shawl was crossed over my chest and pinned to my long gray homespun frock.

It seemed that God called me.

I used to pray, kneeling on the bare stones for long unbroken hours. Sweetness beyond words poured in on me. I felt that all I did was an offering to the great God who gave me everything.

It was said that I was an hysteric. Nothing could be further from the truth. My vision was not the distorted imagination of a girl approaching womanhood and seeking notoriety.

My saints came from Heaven. They spoke to me. They taught me everything. How else could I have learned to lead an army of men into battle?

My life is witness to the power of God to use an untaught peasant girl for special purpose. I was His instrument. All my feats of arms were without meaning unless in obedience to God's command. From Him alone came any virtue I may have had.

I *was* divinely inspired. I *did* see things that others could not see.

I was an untaught country girl, brimful of high spirits and health, whom the King of Heaven chose to fight for France.

Jeanette d'Arc, later called the Maid.

7

CHILDHOOD

I am Jeanne of Domremy, known to the family of d'Arcs as Jeanette. I have descended to earth to speak of my childhood.

My childhood was happy. I grew up amongst men and women used to poverty and toil, and the rearing of many children. We were ill-fed, ill-taught, ill-housed, but our Faith united us. We were pious farmers, and it was a grief to me that I was untaught, when others, not far removed in social rank, could afford to learn the meaning of letters.

I see now that the years I spent at home, doing work on the farm, were as important in God's eyes as the time when I led soldiers. My little family, who lived to please God, were bringing down blessings upon the soil

10

of France. No prayer, no effort, had been lost.

We were superstitious, and used charms and holy water, and prayed before statues. But our arts were entirely innocent and not to be confused with witchcraft, or the invocation of devils, the binding of the will by spell and incantation. I did not know that God would call me Saint, but I did know that He gave me of His spirit, that I might discern the truth. He kept me in His grace, and I obeyed the Church with great exactitude, and was well schooled in all that a Catholic should do and think.

My mother had the indefinable dignity that is beyond class. She was a seer, a healer, a wise woman, gifted with strange gifts.

I too could see. I began to see things that others did not see at that age, and was at first surprised to find that they supposed I was telling lies. I learned to keep my vision private, and distinguish between the things of two worlds.

I saw the Flower Spirits at Easter. The boys carried tapers with tiny yellow banners of flame that puffed out in the wind. The girls carried willow sprays. We processed

11

through Domremy, singing as we went. On entering the church a boy collected the warm smoking tapers in a basket, and we took our places, kneeling on our own little cushions that we carried with us tied by a cord under our arms.

I could not keep my eyes shut. I had to stare at the flowers that my mother had placed on the altar. There were angels behind them. Daisy angels had snow-bright skirts dashed with crimson at the points. The forget-me-nots were blue as jay's feathers, the violets swam in thundercloud purple. Dandelion angels were crowned with fiery crests.

My mother stooped and told me to keep my eyes shut. I was looking at Jesus, with the sprays of green thrust through His thorns, and I thought that He was fortunate to have such lovely angels. I shut my eyes but could see in the dark inside myself.

Everything was scarce—water, candles, thread, needles, oil and salt. All were precious treasures when I was a child. I went with my brothers one day to fill a bucket at the well. We heaved it out and the water gushed over our legs and feet. The boys

12

scolded me and set off bearing it between them, with waves splashing at each step. I trailed behind with the curious sensation that I was on fire. I sat down in a puddle and began to scoop muddy water over my head. When I reached home drowning wet and mud-begrimed, I told my mother that I had been putting out the flames. She thought that I had fallen down the well, and I never went for water again.

I was very nimble on my toes and used to charge up and down the path astride a broomstick, urging my horse forward with whoops and yells. At the age of four I would trot along on sturdy legs to feed the poultry, with my apron full of grain. The ducks and hens mobbed me and tumbled me over. They punched my bare legs full of scarlet beak holes, but I just drove them off pealing with laughter, for I loved birds.

I took a ride in the haycart one summer, and lay in the fragrant hay, powdered in gold dust and tiny blossoms. As I looked up to the blue sea of sky above, a flock of white doves floated down soft as feathers, to throng about me and let me stroke them with my finger. "See Jeanette's white birds," I called to the carter. He turned and tickled me with his whip. "It's jaybirds in the wood," he said. "Don't go telling lies. There's no birds here." There were. I could see them weaving dances and laughing like children as they faded into the clouds.

The priest found me one day in deep conversation with the statue of Michael in Domremy church. I was only telling him how I wished that I had been born a boy, but as I hated farm work, it might not have brought me much fortune. I scampered away and grubbed up a fistful of clover to lay at his feet. The priest told my mother to have a care for my health. I was very queer and odd, but might turn out well if I had proper training.

When I was in the harvest field, at the age of five, I saw an earth fairy. He was stained golden russet like the leaves of early autumn, and had pricky ears like a fox to either side of his furry cap. His lips were deep red, like hawthorn berry, his teeth pointy like a saw blade and milky white. "I am a garner of earth, mademoiselle," he said, making a bow. "I arrange the robes of spring and autumn." His whiskery face was so friendly that I could not be frightened. He was just my height, and I wanted to help him tidy the field of grain, with its crackly stubble full of thistle that hurt my bare legs, but when I looked for him, he had vanished.

I saw a wood elf, or call him what you will, before I was six. I was minding our pigs. They were rooting about in the ferny undergrowth of the oak wood, squeaking like mice. I whistled our dog to round them up to return to sty, when I saw a queer little man in a hazel bush. He was all nut-brown and barky like a tree trunk, all but his merry face. "Mademoiselle Jeanette, I serve the same King, and you will soon be climbing the stairway to His court," I heard him say. I flung down the beechnuts from my apron and ran. The pigs tumbled out of the briers, groveling groutily, with the dog snapping at their heels. I just caught one last glimpse of the brown man. He gave a command and the pigs lined up like soldiers drilling. I thanked him for his kindness, for it spared me much trouble to have obedient pigs.

I could always see the angels and the saints. I watched them lead forth the souls of those slain in battle, just as a child might be led away from the deathbed of its mother. The devils were unable to seize one single soul in my army. Each one of them found mercy and pardon, and the dark spirits who came to suck blood were put to rout. It was the Lady Margaret who made me want to be a man and ride a gray war-horse, with scarlet saddle and shining bit cups.

I would lie awake sometimes, tired though I was, and see the long ladder sloping against the city wall. I would scramble higher and higher, with stones crashing down and arrows whining. I must reach the court of the King, as the fairy said. A soldier ahead of me had been struck. He pitched down head-first into the water of the moat far below. The water swirled around him, like the boiling water in our pot of beans. "O Lady Margaret, take me riding with you," I remember saying to the dim dark empty room. At the sound of my voice, the little sleek mouse dropped his husk, and bobbed back into his hole in the wainscot.

As I grew older, I found that I had a power over animals. When I was very small, I thought it was the fairy folk who were helping me charm birds and drill the sheep. I did not see the little men again, but I often thought of them. At the age of twelve, the saints showed themselves, and I was given the way to calm wild horses, which was very useful knowledge indeed.

I remember Jacques d'Arc saying that if soldiers marched through the village, I must never run after them. My mother said that they had swords to hurt little girls. I must never learn soldiering but help in the house. I said that I would take the spit and chase them, as I chased the fox. He was on his hind legs with his snout between the bars of the hen coop. I would say, "Go away, naughty fox, Jeanette gives the order," and he would trot off with his brush dangling in the dust.

"You are the very last hope left to France, Captain Jeanette," said my mother, smiling, and I took her words to heart.

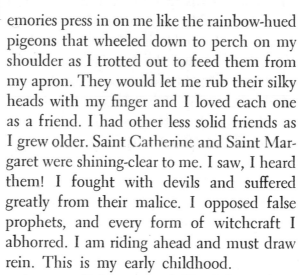

emories press in on me like the rainbow-hued pigeons that wheeled down to perch on my shoulder as I trotted out to feed them from my apron. They would let me rub their silky heads with my finger and I loved each one as a friend. I had other less solid friends as I grew older. Saint Catherine and Saint Margaret were shining-clear to me. I saw, I heard them! I fought with devils and suffered greatly from their malice. I opposed false prophets, and every form of witchcraft I abhorred. I am riding ahead and must draw rein. This is my early childhood.

I was a little young child of five or six, set to snip the grass that bordered the flower beds, with sharp shears. I was breathless with the mighty effort, and instead of grass, I chopped flower heads—dandelion and daisy, and many bright blossoms with names unknown. An idea came to me as I ran the flowers through my fingers and filled my lap. I flung down the shears and ran into the house, to empty my snippings upon the floor. My parents were away and I was alone. I fetched my mother's sewing basket from a shelf. I bit off a length of thread, and found a coarse needle, planning to string a chain. I slit tiny holes in the short stems, poked through a nose of thread and soon had flower heads swinging like washing on a line. Leaving the basket on the floor with bobbins of silk and gilt thread spilling over the rim, I danced away, holding aloft my garland.

I had been forbidden to leave the garden, but I climbed up the gate with no thought other than my great idea. I looked around and I remember nobody was about, except for the farmyard cat with a mouse trailing from her jaws. I knew that I could trust her to keep silent. I ran to the church, and reached the heavy iron-knobbed door. The ring handle was big, cold, stiff and squeaky. I could scarce reach it to turn. The door was ajar. I squeezed inside the dim, dark church with its heavy perfume of rose and lily. I was

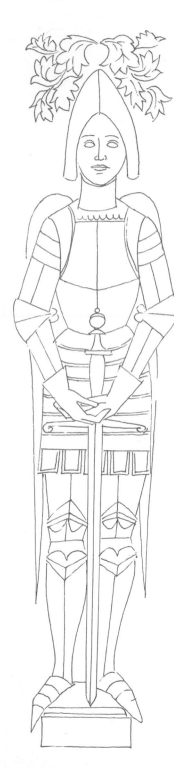

a little frightened, and thought for a moment I would run away, but the beautiful garland I carried made me brave.

I found a small stool that I could stand on, and I dragged it under the tall statue of Saint Michael, climbed up, and flung the garland over his helmet. It slipped to his shoulder, the knot came undone, and the flowers showered in a heap at his feet.

I heard the door open, and cowered back into the shadows beside Saint Michael, terrified and trembling. A man entered.

"Who is there?" came the voice of the priest. He unhooked a tiny lamp, held it aloft. When he saw me, I screamed and tumbled off the stool.

"We will mend your garland, and fetch the Angel more flowers," he said kindly, when I had explained, between my sobs, what I was doing.

Hand in hand we went out of the church to his own garden and gathered a nosegay of beautiful flowers. We returned to the church and set them in a jar before the statue. When the priest had mended the flower crown and made it smaller, he lifted me high, that I might place it on Saint Michael's head.

Hand in hand we returned to my garden.

The priest snipped the grass for me, tidied the bed, and wiped the shears clean on his own sleeve. I saw my mother coming and clung close to him, looking down at the shorn flower stalks with terror.

"Good-day to you, Madame d'Arc," the priest said, smiling sweetly. "Your daughter has been helping me set flowers in the church."

"Will you please to step inside, Father," said my mother. She was dismayed to see her work things all over the floor, and asked if the cat had knocked them down. To my great relief, I saw one of the cat's kits, with a silk bobbin, under the table, but that did not explain the mess of torn petal and leaves.

"I made a garland to put on Saint Michael," I said anxiously, as I saw my mother's face was angry.

"Jeanette made a chain for the Archangel. Perhaps he will wear a dandelion over his heart!" said the priest, and I hugged his arm in raptures of gratitude. My mother fetched him a slice of pigeon pie, as he gathered up the mess with his bare hands, and put it on the fire.

"Well, Father, to contradict would be a blasphemy," my mother said and the episode ended with happiness.

know that I inherited strange gifts from my mother. She was held by many to be a wise woman with the power of healing and fore-knowledge of the future.

I will tell you of an experience I had when I was little more than a child. I came in one evening, cold and wet, and had my work to do before changing into dry clothes. The men had been digging a ditch in the water meadow, and trimming the thorn hedge. They expected food before returning home. I spread a cloth on the trestle table, scoured white as fresh snow with many scrubbings. I pulled up the benches from the wall and laid a platter for each man. I filled the horn mugs with home-brewed herb cordial, then

22

sliced black rye bread, and wafers of rosy bacon from the pig's ham. There was a crumbled yellow cheese veined with green on a wood plate. This and a much-whetted knife and a pot of sweet flowers bedecked the banquet table.

I built up the logs in our ever-burning fire. As I held out my sodden skirt to the flames and watched it steaming, my ears began to sing. I heard a curious humming sound, a soft drone. At first I thought it might be the resin oozing from a gash in the pine log, or a June beetle trapped in a spider web. But it was an unearthly sound, and I trembled and drew closer to the fire.

A voice was saying something. The sound had changed to words. I stood stone-still, listening with every sense alert like a dog at a rabbit's burrow.

"Do not be afraid, Jeanette," I heard in my ears like the sighing of the wind. "I am your mother's father's brother, who fell at Agincourt. You must continue the fight and win back victory for France. You must lead the soldiers to war."

I looked toward the chimney corner and could see nothing, but a man was there quite

close to me. I could have touched him had I struck out my hand.

"I am not allowed to speak with soldiers," I said. "A maid drowned herself for the hurt they had done to her, and they rob our hen-roost and break fences. You are wrong to tell me to lead soldiers. Ask my brothers and perchance they will do so when they have grown."

"No, little Captain Jeanette, I am *not* wrong. I sent you the sound as a warning. We who died at Agincourt will urge you forward. When the time comes you will lead the young men of France."

"Speak with my mother. She will raise an army of the lads of Domremy," I said. "I am too young for war. I have only taken the horse to water. I cannot ride."

"You will ride ahead of all of them, the bravest horseman of France," came the voice, but I heard no more.

The door groaned open on its unoiled hinges. The men came clumping in. They knocked the clay from their clogs on the iron hoop in the porch, and flung down their tools. Then they took their seats at the table, hungry as foxes tearing at a dead

24

goose. I fixed the black pot to the chain up the chimney to heat water, that they might cleanse themselves. Their toil was backbreaking, they said, for the field was sour and the drain blocked with weed roots. They wanted more drink. The bread was finished and the ham carved down to the bone.

One man had a thorn in his thumb, and I had to make a bread-sop and bind it on him. The heat made him squeal. When they had eaten, they carried out the pot of hot water to soak their blistered feet in the trough in the shed. They were grateful in their rough way. They thanked me for what I had done and left me to clear up.

I gathered the greasy platters in a basket and collected the rinds of bacon to boil for broth. I wiped the grease from the table and swept the floor. It was only then that I realized how weary I was. I stretched out my naked feet to the bright flame, watching the sparks flung high like a handful of tossed coins. I thought of our men with their loud laughs and ungainly strides. They would not make very skilled soldiers to fight for France. They would be braver than I, but who could train them?

see again the long, low, smoke-blackened
room where we worked and ate. I used to
card the fleece into silky-soft clouds of wool,
with sharp-toothed combs before spinning.
We made our cloth and dyed it from roots
and bark. Usually it was a gray, black or
russet brown. The natural pale cream of
sheep wool was thought a luxury as it needed
much laundering to keep it clean, and besides, our own sheep were a grizzled gray.

Our garments had constantly to be repaired. As we worked by the fireside, patch-
ing and mending, we used to sing. My
mother worked thread with bone needles, I
patched and darned. My father would mend

harness, plait and cobble, splice a rope, or hammer away at a broken tool. Our lives were full of toil.

A terrible pestilence claimed many of our strongest men. When the men fell sick, the women had to work in the fields to keep their families alive, taking with them the young children to do what work they could. Our village cast leaves like trees in a gale, and the churchyard was bursting full of freshly dug graves. My mother went from house to house to comfort the dying and prepare food for the aged. Scores of unburied corpses were left to rot in every ditch. Children died.

I have a last memory of the pestilence, that spared the members of my own household but not those who worked for us.

Our aged shepherd tottered back to us, his hands quivering, his face green and lined like a crushed petal, to tell us that God was punishing France for sin. I went with him to help him pen the sheep and he told me to tarry a moment for he was gasping for breath. He drew from beneath his smock a bundle of bone spindles, carved at the top with little grinning human heads. He said

27

they had been handed down from father to son. By their aid he could read the future. He laid them in a pattern on the grass and he said—I remember so well what he said— he said he saw devils tossing fireballs from the clouds that tumbled towns to touch-wood.

My mother came and scolded us for not being at work, but her eyes softened when she looked at the shepherd's pain-wrinkled face.

He died that night. He left my mother a box that contained his few treasures. We shook them out on the table—pebbles, buttons, foreign coins, dice and grains of sweet-scented gum. My mother put a finger to the carven roses on the lid. As she did, there came a click and a secret door shot open. I saw the little men, with caps and crowns and wicked leering faces. She said the figurines were devil's toys, and she wrapped them in a rag and made me fling them in a pond.

That night, as I lay in bed, it seemed to me the tiny men and women came alive. They crowded around me to grin and chatter and wag their painted heads. The bony king,

with his gilded crown, pointed a thin finger
at me and said he would divine my future,
and they laughed and danced and screamed
like a flock of magpies. I bade them begone,
and buried my head in the blanket. I said
that I gave my future to God and they
should not read it. It was nothing to them
what I did. They must lie in the pond where
they had fallen. Their mocking laughter
grew faint and I fell asleep.

During the drought summer, my brother
fished them out, pale and wan, with the
paint gone from their faces. He hid them
in the woodshed, divining idols of a bygone
age, but they hid their secret and never
troubled me again.

The King, the Courtier, the Page, the
Doctor, the Devil, the Angel, the Fool, I
met them all, later, in real life.

hen I was perhaps ten years old, my mother took me to a horse fair, together with my brothers and sisters, that we might sell our produce. It was held in a green meadow by the river. Besides the sale of horse and foal, there were sports and sideshows, tilting, archery and other delights. All of us loved to visit a fair, to see the wagons decorated with garlands, and the proud horses with ribbons plaited through their manes. I loved to watch the crooked-legged colts, wagging their lamb's-wool tails and thrusting at their dams' flanks with neat little velvet muzzles. Horses were my great delight. I watched them racing on the turf, and longed with all my heart to sit astride them.

I remember this particular day, when we

arrived at the fair, my sisters went to watch a pageant, my brothers scampered off to see the wrestling, my father sold produce at our market stall. I held my mother's hand, lest I lose her in the crowd, and we went to see the performing dogs. I wanted to try my luck at dart throwing and spinning a ball to knock down wooden soldiers, but I had no money to spare on such things. We came to a gay tent, striped blue and white with a painted sign. It showed the palm of a hand, crossed and recrossed with golden lines. My mother said it was a palmist's booth. She had heard that they told marvelous things, but we were poor and could not afford to go in. Tinkers used to camp in the green lanes near Domremy, filling pan holes with melted tin, tracing palms, drawing teeth and doctoring horses.

This very gypsy had knocked on our door and my mother had given her food. I recognized her tilted cart and the spotted roan snatching grass on a tether, behind the tent. We had been told that she was a Bohemian of noble birth. Her husband had gambled away their fortune and left her destitute to read hands or starve. I begged my mother to let me have my hand read, and said the palmist would reduce her price. I begged and tormented her and, at last, my mother grudgingly agreed.

We found ourselves inside the striped tent, face to face with a beautiful woman. The palmist was tall and commanding, with high cheekbones, burning brown eyes, and brows blackened with a paintbrush. Her throat was chained around with dancing golden coins which jingled as she moved. She wore a laced bodice, heavily encrusted with silver specks of metal, and wide sleeves embroidered richly. Her skirts were of costly brocade. I stared at her in wonderment, then rummaged in my smock and brought out a few sticky coins to lay on the table.

The palmist said they were not enough, but then she recognized my mother and her face was wreathed in smiles. She said she would read my mother's hands for what I had paid. I licked my palms and rubbed them clean as I watched the woman examining every crease in my mother's toil-scarred hands with great intensity. She turned them back and front, examined the nails and joints, and measured the span.

"You were called to dedicate your life to a sisterhood, but a great misfortune changed your destiny," the palmist said at last. "I see the wolves of want baring their teeth, but a bright flame comes upon you and drives them back. I smell burning, but wait—your prayers fall down, not as gold pieces but as gold threads that form a robe to protect you. You have the hand of a holy woman, but it is torn and scarred with fear and trouble. The loss of something you love is very close."

"Thank you. The tent is very hot. I think we will go," my mother said. "You may have heard scraps of gossip when you camped at Domremy."

"Stay," said the palmist, and the coins around her neck winked their sparks, illumined by the little lamp that hung from the king pole of the tent. She put my money in her bodice, and then tilted up my face to observe it with her jewel-bright eyes.

I was a little frightened, and hid my hands behind my back. I did not now want them to be read. I could not say why. She pulled both my hands forward and forced back my clenched fingers, holding them close in her own strong white palms.

33

"Madame d'Arc," she said, "your child is not of this earth. Very soon she will be leaving it."

My mother tried to laugh. "Jeanette is very much *in* the earth, if not *of* it," she said, pointing to the grassy smears on my smock. "She is a good girl, but no angel, and you must not turn her head by your fancies. Jeanette must labor to win bread, whatever her hand may read."

My mother took me by the arm and tried to hurry me out, but the palmist gripped my shoulder. Her pointy nails bit into me like bird claws and she dragged me back.

"I must look again at your daughter's hand. I read her fate in the air over her head." The palmist broke out into a foreign gibberish, full of strange words, as she struggled with me. She was very strong and she forced open my right hand and examined it again closely. Suddenly she gave a cry and dropped it.

"Gracious God, what a hand is this, Madame d'Arc," she said excitedly. "Your daughter, Jeanette, was born for a throne." She tried to kiss my fingers, and tears ran down her gaunt cheeks.

The tent walls bulged inward from the press outside, for we had outstayed our time. Two goose-faced, giggling girls pushed inside, unasked. They were impatient to hear of their future sweethearts, and told us to be gone. The palmist was moaning, her face held between her long white fingers.

"I have never seen such a sign in all my readings—never, never! You must bring Jeanette again, with a piece of silver. I have seen something in her hand that makes me tremble. I have seen a terrible crown. Oh, Madame d'Arc, I must read your daughter's fortune again. She has the rarest sign within it that the hand can have."

She bent down and whispered in my mother's ear, but I heard her.

"Oh, Madame d'Arc, she has the *double cross*!"

Somehow we tumbled ourselves out of the tent into the clean sunlight and hurried across the grass to find Jacques d'Arc. The cart was harnessed ready. He was fretting to be away. I looked back to see the fortune-teller's tent being closed. The palmist had put a sign outside—a man standing before a shuttered window with outstretched arms.

My father had sold his produce, my sisters had won an ornamental vase, my brothers had won a sports prize and were very happy. I looked at my hand wonderingly, but the creases meant nothing to me. It was a strong, sun-baked child's hand that hid its secrets. I said I had been to the palmist and my father was angry. I should have been beside him selling vegetables. Only knaves and vagabonds peddled palms.

My mother had turned very pale, and I feared the sun had been too much for her. She said brokenly, at last, that it was all nonsense. There was nothing in my hand that could be read. We had just gone to the tent for a little fun on a fair day. It was nonsense for a child my age to learn about her future. She herself knew what it contained—life on a farm with many children.

y mother, Isabeau Romée, was of Norman stock and very pious. She had been brought up with nuns, and had more learning than the other poor folk of the village that had become her home. Every summer she went on pilgrimage to a nearby shrine that held an ancient statue of the holy Virgin.

The pilgrims were usually poor. We had to make many sacrifices to afford the journey and have a small sum in reserve to give as alms. I will tell of my first pilgrimage with her. It was midsummer and very hot. We drove together in a farm cart hired for the journey. We were a merry party. We sang and joked as we jolted on, accompanied by a vast crowd of pilgrims, on foot or on horse, in barrows and litters and tilted carts, all making their way to the shrine. There they would make petitions and receive healing. They would pray for an end to the sufferings our land endured.

We arrived at the inn where we were to spend the night. I laid out my clean robe upon the bed, took off my shoes to wash my feet, and unpacked the comb, to struggle with my unruly hair. My mother had a stiff white, freshly laundered coif for her head. She rubbed the grime from her cheeks with a rag dipped in a basin of cold water.

The tall curtained bed that we were to share looked none too clean, and the walls of the attic were broken and disfigured by drawings. Somebody had sketched a battle scene, with bodies spouting crimson gore, and archers hurling bolts from their crossbows. There was a moat below the walls splashed in green and blue, full of drowned men. As I stared at the picture, there was a knock at the door, and the innkeeper came in to say that it was time to join the party going to the shrine.

"Admiring my painting, girl?" he said to me. "An artist fellow left here owing rent, and I took his paints for payment. Battle breaks us and church mends us. I livened up the wall a bit to hide the stains."

"I wish I could paint like you, monsieur," I said enviously, though the men were spider thin or bolster fat, with shapeless turnip heads.

"You shall have a try at it, on the clean bit of white boarding by the window. I have his brushes and paint pans. If it is bad, I will whiten it out with the wash left from the byre. You shall do the Virgin sending healing. Very fitting for the pilgrims to see." He left us.

There was something about the battle that riveted my attention. I felt a wave of sorrow go through me at sight of the poor bodies spouting blood, as I felt my own young flesh, firm and pulsing with the strength of youth. I wanted to bind the wounds, and send the hated English running like rats from a burning rick.

Anger and sorrow filled me as I proceeded to church, holding tightly to my mother, pressed and jostled by the ragged, dirty, evil-smelling swarm of sick and suffering.

The Virgin's shrine was very crowded, and there was scarce room to kneel. Prayer went up ceaselessly. There were cries, groans, muttered sorrows, as the herd of supplicants made known their needs. The wounded lay on pallets, cheese-colored and fainting. Mothers held up little shrunken babes, as yellow as the toads in the hedge, with swollen bellies and twisted limbs. Waves of blue incense floated and spiraled, but the rose and lily sweetness could not drown the stench of sweat and rotting flesh, warm iron and charred wick.

I watched the glowing wick of my little white taper wink, tumble in a squash of melted wax with a crackle and a puff of black woolly smoke. I thought this must be a sign that God had rejected my prayer that I might heal the poor soldiers spouting blood. The holy Virgin in her dim dark alcove was too busy to hear my prayer. I was alone and forgotten.

My mother was praying beside me with her hands clasped to her bosom, her eyes tight shut. I got to my feet, squeezed through the crowd, and my going was not noticed. There was the drone of voices from the High Altar, and I felt very guilty to be leaving church at such a holy time.

I sat down on the grass behind a tombstone. The air was fresh and good. I must go to the war and heal wounds, I thought to myself. I would hide in one of the wagons and go to the war. Surely the Virgin would grant my prayer when she saw that I was in earnest.

I saw a cripple with a leg stump fixed to a wood crutch, and offered help. He swore a fearful oath. He told me to skip off on the legs I still had, or he'd break them for me. I went up to an old woman, her face covered with sores, her arm with ulcers, and said I would dress them with the grease used for lambing that I carried in my sack. I smoothed on the melted hog fat, and made her a sling from my kerchief. She waved me away without thanks and was swallowed up in the crowd. A soldier stood beside me, his head swathed in blood-soaked towels. I looked up into his face imploringly but hesitated, as I was strictly forbidden to speak to men from the battlefields.

"Buy a lucky medal," said a voice, and I looked down at a horrible hunchback dwarf, with a tray of charms on his chest. I had given away my kerchief, with my only coin

41

tied to the hem. I gazed sadly at his twisted purple face, and said I had no money.

"You have the gold of God around you if not the silver of earth," he said, and he gave me a medal in exchange for a little wood cross. "Let us beg together, sweet lady. Your good face will change my fortunes. We will pick up a living going from fair to fair. How come you to be so alone in such a throng?"

"The holy Virgin was angry, so I left the church," I said, "but let me go back and pray. Perhaps she will make you tall and straight."

"That can never be," answered the dwarf. "My mother was the servant at a grand house, and I am the bastard of a rich lord. She took herbs to kill me before I saw the light of day, and I was born crooked. I can only keep alive by being so. You must not heal me."

We sat down on a log. I gave him a slice of meat done up in a cabbage leaf that I had for my evening meal. He ate it greedily. I could see his pointy elbows sticking from his ragged coat and felt like weeping. As I fingered the tin medal of the Virgin tied around my neck by a thread, I had an idea.

"Rest here," I said. "I will beg for you.

When we have collected some money, you shall come back to the inn and buy a meal. Perhaps you could come home with us. Then I will go to the war as a beggar and gather money for the dying men. If they wear the medals, they will get well of their wounds."

My dreams were shattered by my mother's hauling me to my feet and cuffing me. She was in a terrible state of nerves, and she shouted at me as she dragged me to the inn. She had been searching up and down the place. I was a wicked girl to have run away.

I was left in the bedroom to sob my heart out, whilst she attended Vespers.

I found the jars of color and a thin painting brush the innkeeper had left for me. I began to paint. The whitening on the wall sucked up my color and blurred the outline, but I sketched the figure of the Virgin with hands outstretched in healing. I took a taper from the wall bracket and set out to kindle it in the fire belowstairs. I would burn a candle to her. This time perchance my prayer would be granted.

As I entered the servants' quarters I heard a great commotion. A fight was going on between the potboy and the ugly dwarf. His tray was upside down, and the little bright medals were scattered over the floor.

"I'll teach you to come selling lucky medals and stealing the cat's dinner," raged the cook, a stout puffy woman, armed with a frypan. "Get out of our kitchen, you horrible creature," screamed a pantry maid, flinging a handful of peelings.

"Run, run for your life," I said. The dwarf and I ran out the back door into the courtyard, with a hail of eggshells and cabbage stalks flying through the air behind us. We dodged behind the carts and hid until the chase died down. Then we slipped out in the lane, squeezed through a hedge, and sat down in a field.

"I am ruined," lamented the dwarf, as he gnawed a collop of beef he had stolen from the inn.

"We will sell lucky posies instead," I told him. I gathered some blossoms from the hay grass and twisted them into small bunches. We stood in the church porch, selling nosegays to the pilgrims. A lady emptied her purse into his cupped hands. He put the coins in the lining of his peaked cap and danced a jig.

"You have the gold of Heaven all about you," he said again. "The medal of the Virgin has brought you fortune already. You can give me your belt to strap the pack with." He took it from me.

It was then my mother found me, as she came out from prayer.

When I arrived home from pilgrimage, my father thrashed me. I had lost my kerchief and belt and also my sack—for so it had proved. I had run away from my mother and taken up with a most notorious cutpurse dwarf. The innkeeper had charged for whitening out my picture. I was in disgrace.

I had grown in stature by the experience. I felt that I was no longer a child. I prayed as I had never prayed, in our own Domremy church, laying my cheek against the cold feet of the Virgin and pouring out my heart.

"O blessed Mary," I said to her, "let me be your servant. Send me to your soldiers with red blood streaming out of them, to make them well again. For the sake of the medal I wear in your honor, give me your blessing that I may give to others. Oh please answer my prayer."

was in the harvest field, twisting the straw bands to bind the corn shocks, when I seemed to hear a voice calling me. The men were seated under a shady tree taking their brief rest in the noonday heat. They were munching bread and drinking sour wine from the big flagon I had carried for them. I heard a voice calling me from high in the cloudless sky, higher than the lark. It came, I supposed, from the golden-faced sun itself.

"Jeanette," said the voice, "I need your service."

"What may I do to please you, sire?" I said politely, dropping on my knees on the sharp prickly stubble, gazing into the blue but seeing no one.

"I will you to save France."

46

"That would I gladly do, sire, but I am hard pressed with the harvest."

"I have chosen you, Jeanette, and will speak with you again."

I waited and counted my heartbeats, and looked all around me. Then I got to my feet and watched the glossy corn spikes straightening their backs slowly.

There was no angel to be seen, but the sweet-toned voice had been real. I felt a great urge shake me, a compelling certainty, that nothing in later years could ever shatter. God had called me.

The men were on their feet, and we went on working, tying the waist of each corn bunch with a twisty rope of straw, and leaning the shocks upright in clumps of four, like children kissing. I was said to handle the shocks as bravely as a lad of older years. This made me so vain that I worked the harder.

Shortly after this, my parents were visited by the preaching friar who heard me in confession. He said that I confessed with ardor, and showed such inclination for the path of holiness, he thought that a life within a sisterhood was my vocation. My parents opposed the scheme. Jacques d'Arc said I was

a strong girl and that he could not spare
me on the farm. My mother said that it
would be unwise to part with me. She had
a good husband in view and all had been
arranged.

I was bitterly disappointed, for I would
have loved to become a nun. I searched for
consolation and guidance, but for a while
I found no answer. The voice did not call
from Heaven. My little wood crucified one
bore his pain in silence. I asked Jesus to
show me what I must do. I prayed, but there
was silence. Silence so complete and lasting
that the joy I had felt within the harvest field
turned to pain. I had my share of rough fa-
tiguing labor. Jacques d'Arc said that I had
come to my senses, and he was devoutly
thankful.

He came to me in the field of furrow,
when I was all bedaubed in clay. Hard fi-
brous roots had entangled themselves in the
plow colter. I jerked the reins to halt the
oxen, and started to free the blade with a
pointed stick. I tore away the gouts of earth
with my bare hands. What was hindering
the plow? It refused to move. I beat the lazy

oxen with the reins, and called Heigh-o, the
signal to go forward. I grasped the handles
and tried to steady the plow. I looked back
at the frill of clod, sliced clean like new
bacon, and forward to the ungrooved por-
tion. The women had not cleared the stones,
the field was barren and sour, but the plow
was well greased and newly sharpened.

"Go on!" I commanded, and hit the oxen
on their buttocks. They leaned to the yoke,
then trumpeted through wide nostrils and
began to tremble.

I felt a tingling sensation run down my
spine. My blue chilblained hands prickled
and burned. It was then I saw him. A man
was standing on the furrow a lance length
from me, young, smiling, and well fashioned. I stared. The instant before, I had
been alone in a half-plowed field. I stared
but was not affrighted. He wore his silken
brown hair long and it stirred in the breeze.
He had a blue cloak that deepened to violet
in the creases. He wore armor according to
the mode of the time, but he was not of
earth, my heart told me.

"Do not fear, Mademoiselle Jeanette. I
come from Heaven to be your friend," he

said, and his face was ablaze with light and friendliness. I smoothed the ragged sack that served for apron, and dropped a curtsy.

"Sire, you do me honor, but who are you? I would know first." I did know already that he was no devil.

"I am Prince Michael, Captain of the Angels. I have come to tell you that God has chosen you to do a mighty work for France."

Joy set my spirits churning like water in a millrace, and a cry tumbled out of me, like lark song, because no power can stem it.

"O sire, I am ready. When the plowing is done, it will be near dark and tomorrow I must arise before dawn. My tasks are never finished, but what lies in me to do, that will I willingly do to please God."

"I will come to you again," said the Prince. He told me other things and the plow was forgotten. When he left me, the oxen, shaken like birds in a gale, heaved so that I could scarce control them. I went on plowing, unheeding of its merit, but when I came to finish I found that I had steered aright without bungling the corners.

When I began to clean the plow that

night, it burned my hands. It made them tingle as if nettles stung me, but it was pleasing warmth, alive and comforting. I gripped the handles again and again to be sure. Then, scarce taking measure of aught around me, I staggered into my home and fell asleep in the chimney corner.

Michael came to me again, of course, many times. I grew to love him dearly.

O Michael, Michael, Captain of the Angel Host, God's leader, it was for your sweet sake I left my home and entered battle. I chose sword and buckler, war-horse and spurs. For you I ordered armies, I broke the siege of war, I tumbled towers. For you I bled, I charged forward, I triumphed and prevailed, I fell, I entered the flames.

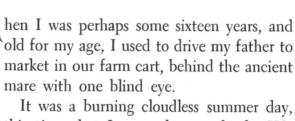

hen I was perhaps some sixteen years, and old for my age, I used to drive my father to market in our farm cart, behind the ancient mare with one blind eye.

It was a burning cloudless summer day, this time that I remember so clearly. We rolled and rumbled over the stony track. Huddled under a net in the well of the cart were terrified and noisily lamenting sheep, together with the strings of onions and turnips and cabbages tied in a sack, that we hoped to sell.

We reined up in the cobbled square of the small market town, let down the tailboard of the cart, and drove the sheep inside the wattled pen we had hired. We were surrounded by noise and clamor. Farmers

52

shouted as they herded their pigs and poultry. The air shook with the vibrant wailing
of cows torn from their calves, and of frightened foals the men were beating. We had
with us a raw farm lad who had run behind
the cart on foot. Jacques d'Arc, who was hot
and thirsty, told him to mind the pen and
sell every sheep whilst he went to the Tra-
veler's Rest for a mug of ale. The crowd of
purchasers had not had time to assemble,
coming as they did from faraway hamlets
and farms.

We had leisure to refresh ourselves before
the sale began. We left the little ragged lad
weeping, sitting inside the pen with the
sheep, examining his blistered feet. I forced
my way through the surging crowd of
vendors and drove into the yard of a nearby
inn. I unfastened the traces and led out the
bony mare, and tied her to a ring. Hung over
her bridle was a bag of chaff to comfort her.
The horseboy offered to clean the cart, but
my father said tartly that he like it caked
with clay.

We went into the inn taproom. On market days it was thronged with farmers who
liked to share complaint and gossip. They

commented gloomily on the price of barley, the outrage done by soldiers, the sad state that France was in. My father complained of the price of wheat. Times were bad, he said. France was wounded and about to die for nccd of hclp.

The beamed room was long and low, with a trestle table down the center and benches to either side. Over the arched chimney corner hung long sharp oxhorns, wired to the beam. There was a mouse-eaten stuffed otter on a shelf, a battle-ax and a dented helmet.

We sat down at the table. My father drew his knife and whetted it on his boot, and began to twist a roll of bread. The board was patterned with tankard circles, crude scrawlings of women's heads and hearts wounded by arrow bolts, to tell of the agony of love. The bench was lined with rosy-brown farmers. They brayed and snorted like the cattle in the square, bubbled and slopped their ale, and rocked with laughter at their own jokes. They gobbled and chomped, blew out their lips and unlaced their smocks, strained to bursting over their gross paunches.

A serving maid placed a platter of bacon meat before me, but the noise and stench made my ears sing. I had no taste for the yellow fat. I drank the bitter herb drink. My father was telling of our tame jackdaw. It went berry picking perched on his shoulder, pricking the choicest fruit from his cupped hand. I sat unnoticed—a rough sheepherder with red blistered hands, her head tied in a kerchief, her smock worn and threadbare.

My eyes roamed. A small lad licked his platter, and his father knocked his knuckles with a spoon. A sheep dog balanced on his hunkers, and I slipped him my meat. The maid was perched on a farmer's knee, squawling like a porker as he tickled her. Then I became aware of the blue-eyed stranger.

The man who had squeezed in beside me was unlike the other tavern drinkers. He was slender, well-looking, very brown and sweet-scented and well-stitched like a new bridle of Spanish leather. He had broad shoulders inside his tight plum-colored cloth jerkin. His waist was tightly girthed. Suddenly he turned and looked at me and smiled a merry smile. It crinkled up his friendly face and made it warm and sunlit. His eyes were very white and very blue. They rested on me with interest, as though I were a flower, not a plow girl.

"You are not eating, mademoiselle," he said in a low voice. He slipped a little cake onto my knee from the pouch at his belt.

"I am a little tired by lifting the sheep from the cart, but it is nothing," I said, and I began to nibble at the honey cake hidden in my hand.

He was such a fine, strong-looking young man, I marveled that he was not in the army. He seemed too gracious and nobly born to be in such rough company. He read my thoughts.

"I am not a soldier yet, mademoiselle. I am the son of a mercer. I was apprenticed to a cloth merchant, and I ran away. I won a little money at a gaming table, and I became a courier, because of my speed at running. When I fought a duel and was set in irons, I ran for my life, not for daily bread. When I have recovered from a wound, I will run again. Where do you live? I would like to visit you."

I shook my head. "I am kept strictly, monsieur. I work on a farm. I am Jeanette d'Arc of Domremy, the shepherdess."

"I am Martel the runner, and I will visit you." He touched my knee under the table. "I am an inventor, mademoiselle. I have made a design for a cannon that can hurl a ball straight, without leaping into the air or cracking from heat. It will be the way of winning the war, but I need gold to have it cast at a foundry. I must have it made. My great cannon, drawn by six shining black stallions, shall be a present for the Prince. How can I find gold?"

The attention he showed me I felt strangely disturbing. The intense earnestness of his manner made me forget all else. Our heads bent close and I forgot the noise around me beating upon the air like blows from an anvil. I took no heed of the swilling half-drunk farmers, making coarse jest, banging the table and spilling ale. Before my eyes I saw the fireballs crashing into the forts, the cannon spouting plumes of fire.

"Do a thing for God's glory, and the sun will shine on you, monsieur," I found myself saying. "I will ride our shire horse to the captain at arms and tell him of the cannon.

Our own armorer, the iron smith at Domremy, will fashion it."

"I must first have gold."

"No, Monsieur Martel, you must bless the idea and harness angel power to your will and it will grow wings. Our young pigeons are a bag of bent bone, with hair like wet grass, but I sprinkle gold grains for them and they plump out. They turn patchwork color like a dawn sky. They flap off and beat out the young barley with their wings. They find what gold they want."

"Mademoiselle, you are right! I will marshal my ideas like young soldiers and drive them forth, well drilled and in battle array, to dig for iron. My cannon must come to birth like a great winged dragon."

"The lump of iron is a poor cold dead thing until the blacksmith warms it scarlet red, and hoops and fashions it. I can hear the blows falling like chiming bells, as our smith beats the horseshoe to batter the flints to fire. Oh, monsieur," I said, "the lords and ladies will give us gold. I will stand in the market square and plead for it."

As I looked into his eyes, I thought of all the blue things I loved—June sky, harebells, and jay feathers. He touched my hand with his brown fingers and warmth flooded me.

"I will tell you a secret," he said, whispering into my ear. "A man from the East looked into my palm. He told me that I could make and make. He said that when I met will and purpose knit together in one, found someone who could batter down rebelliousness so that one sole desire lived within them, God would set a light to the idea. Then I could not fail. God can make dead things alive, if all that opposes His purpose is trampled down. You have given me the answer to my quest."

There was silence. I looked up to see the eyes of the rough crowd fixed upon us. There was a bellow of laughter that made me feel very uncomfortable.

"When you have mastered yourself, Jeanette, perhaps you will harness the cart," said my father, scowling.

"Our Jeanette needs the spur," mocked a farmer.

"I'll master her with my whip," laughed another.

I climbed over the bench with my cheeks burning, and ran out of the room.

The horseboys leaned against the cart, chewing straws, unwilling to serve a farm girl. I backed the mare between the shafts and shackled the traces unaided. The horse collar sprouted straw like a bird nest, the reins were spliced with cord, the cart was cracked like a pond in drought. I ran my hand under the girth and found a sprig of thorn had been placed there in prank. With what dignity I could muster, I told a groom to give a lick of tar to the mare's hooves. As I flung him the only coin I had, I felt a touch on my arm. The blue-eyed stranger was beside me.

"You are the great discovery, Mademoiselle d'Arc," he said to me. "In you meets the will and the purpose to win the battle of France. You are my great invention, made in flesh. The cannon of my dreams."

"My life is set and I am chained," I answered sadly.

"Turn the furniture around the other way, and open the window of your heart, mademoiselle. Call back your pigeons full of golden grain . . ."

I did not want to leave him. I looked appealingly into his face, thinking for an instant that he would carry me away with him. My father, very red in the face and angry with the heat, was climbing into the cart.

"Hurry, you lazy turnip head," he shouted, to the delight of the horseboys.

"Good-bye, Monsieur Martel," I said, as I perched on the shafts and gathered the reins. "A brood of little ones will be the ideas that will come to me. My life is fixed to a shape I cannot alter."

The cart was moving, but he ran beside me and caught the hem of my smock.

"You are wrong, mademoiselle," he cried in a ringing voice that all could hear. "You will make of yourself a shrine. And be the well-beloved of all the world, God's darling."

I wanted to smack his face for being forward, but Jacques d'Arc struck the mare on the rump with his stick. We jarred the door lintel with our wheel hub as the mare leaped forward with a brief show of spirit.

Our sheep had escaped and the little lad had gone in chase of them.

Every market day that followed, I went without refreshment and was left to guard them. Every day until I became a soldier.

am Jeanne the Maid. I have descended to earth and visited the cathedral where my Liege Lord was crowned. I gazed up at the jeweled window above the High Altar. The colored patchwork of glass winked like dragon eyes in the warm sunlight. I bowed myself in prayer. It seemed the glorious warrior, the Angel Michael, was standing before me, wings outspread. I remembered how he first came to me, as I drove the plow oxen. I held the handles of the plow with numb red fingers, a ragged shawl crossing my breast, my leathern apron bedaubed in clay. It is ever my desire to serve him. I wear France as a robe about my person. Her sorrows wound me, her joys console me, and every prayer said to me, I lift to God.

The history books say that I wore a red robe when I went to the Captain de Baudricourt. It is of this robe that I would speak.

I was a young girl, and had gone with my parents to market, in a nearby town. It was a good day. We sold our produce profitably. As a rare treat, my mother promised me yarn to weave a robe for saint days. There was a shop well known to me, adjoining the market square, where goods were displayed on a counter under a striped awning. I approached the stall with the coins tied in a corner of my kerchief.

It was closing time. The lad in charge was shoveling the unsold goods through the open window at the rear, before folding up the booth for the night.

"Stay a moment," I said to the boy. "I want a hank of red weft to lay over our warp of natural sheep wool."

I had set my heart on a bright red, different from the russet and gray that the village maidens wore, home-dyed from bark and berry.

"Closing down. All sold out," said the boy, struggling with the heavy bales.

"I will have a skein of that rose-red and four of the blue," I said, undaunted. "We have been good customers and I have a basket to take them away." I smiled my most winning smile.

The boy laughed.

"We are closed, mademoiselle, and there is not enough red or blue left. You would need to add green and brown and yellow. The girls will mock to see you go to Mass in many colors like a butterfly." He pushed the last bale of cloth through the open window at the back of the booth and slammed the shutter.

I was angry at his rudeness and more than ever determined to buy my wool. I dived under the trestle counter and caught him by the arm.

"Take me to your lady and I will buy from her," I said with the same authority I used on the sheep dogs.

He hesitated and grumbled, but ended by obeying. He led me to the rear of the shop and we entered the workroom. I found myself in a rafted shed, piled high with bales and bundles, and bee skeps, bobbins and hanks of thread, spindles and broken looms and saddlery. An old woman with a fierce hawklike face was spinning at a wheel. The boy bowed and touched his forelock.

"It's the sheep girl from Domremy, madame. Says she won't be put off with it being closing time. She must have some yarn." He scowled.

"Pardon me, madame," I said. "You have often bought our fleece and I have come today to buy yarn for a robe. I have been hard at work selling and could not come before. I will take five skeins and go."

"You are very determined," said the old woman. "You may purchase a length of the rose-red cloth by your side. Pierre shall shear it, and it costs three crowns an ell."

I fingered the soft material enviously, but shook my head. It was far too costly for me, fitting only for a grand lady of fashion. I gazed around the room admiring the rainbow-hued yarns and rich brocades, and decided that I must and would have a red dress. I wanted to peel off a skin from the sunset and be arrayed in glory, but there was no red stuff that I could afford. I could buy sheep raddle and dye the wool myself, or crush poppies, or boil rowan berries, but red, blood red, was the color I desired and meant to have.

"Russet, or natural gray with a black cape, would be more in keeping with a girl of your sort," said the fierce old woman, fixing me with her bird-bright eyes, mocking at me.

"I will have the one red skein to knit myself mittens, and good-day to you madame. I am sorry to have been of trouble," I said as I counted out coins in my hand.

The old woman continued to survey me with her piercing gaze. The lad, having put the skein in my basket, opened the door and made a jerky gesture for me to be gone.

"One moment, please," said the woman in a commanding voice. I stopped. "My young sheepherder, you have a compelling way with you, and I have taken a fancy to your looks. You have chosen red to cover you, when all others would have chosen clay color or earth brown. I have an idea. My life is well-nigh over, and yours spreads ahead, like a dawn sky changing from gray to rose. My son's young bride died of the fever. The robe I gave her is in the press. Fetch it, Pierre. I will make you a gift of it. The thing makes my heart ache."

Pierre unhooked the robe from its peg inside an oaken press, and shook out the rich cloth, from inside its windings of linen. The woman held the dress against me, and it dropped and fell like a blush rose, full of beautiful color. I tore off my smock and put it on. It fell around me in waves and crinkles of crimson color, so that I gasped with pleasure. It was flared at the back to form a train. The sleeves were far too long and hung over my hands in a red droop. The old woman drew in the latchet threads under the armpits and buckled me tightly under the breasts. The robe fitted. She took her shears and snipped away a hand's span about my feet, and turned back the pointed cuffs. A sweet scent of lavender and gums was all about me. The cloth had the soft texture of a ripe velvet peach. I stroked my sleek sides and strutted up and down, unable to speak.

"Fold it carefully in the sheet, and tie it with cord for the customer," said the old woman. "It reminds me of the sweet young bride who wore it but once. It might be dyed in heart's blood. With it goes my pain."

I did not know how to thank her for my most wondrous gift, but I mumbled out some incoherent words of gratitude. Clasping my precious bundle to my chest, I ran from the room.

"What have you got in that bundle?" said my mother sharply, as we trundled along homeward. The battered old farm cart swayed over the ruts like a ship in a gale.

"I have been given the most beautiful dress, like the rubies in a church window. Look, Mother, look!" I said. I shook out the red robe over the coop of lusty young cockerels crowing in the well of the cart. My mother gave a cry.

"You must take that dress back at once," she said, her face as white as milk.

"But, Mother, I can't, I can't," I protested. "She gave it me with her blessing. A robe for saints' days, for my very own. I have never seen such a lovely color to suit me. I could never take it back. She would not have it."

"You can, and she will," said my mother, in a tone of voice strange to me. "That robe holds some of the woman who last wore it. Her life must not touch yours. You must never wear it, Jeanette. We will take it back now."

Nothing would change her purpose. Jacques d'Arc, swearing angrily, had to turn the horse and drive back to the town.

We arrived at the shop to find a battle in progress. Pierre had left some bobbins on the counter when he took me behind it, and they had been stolen. Boys had hooked them through the latticed shutter in front of the booth. The shopkeeper was belaboring Pierre with a spindle, shrieking that he was a thief. Sobbing bitterly I returned the robe. She hit me on the head and called me bad names, and said that I had brought a curse with me. She grabbed the skein of red wool from my basket, and drove me out with a kick.

I visited the town the next year. I went to the shop with a basket of eggs as a gift. At closing time, Pierre was fixing the shutters in place. He put out his tongue at me. I made him take me to the rear of the shop. There was the gray-haired woman at her tall spinning wheel.

"The thief that stole the red robe, come again," said Pierre, digging me in the ribs with his elbow.

To my surprise, the spinner greeted me with a friendly smile.

"Be welcome, my daughter," she said sweetly. "I was angry with you, Mademoiselle Jeanette, but out of grief springs joy. See what my robe has done for me."

From a settle in the chimney corner, a young girl arose and came to greet me. She was rose-dappled, fresh and soft, like apple blossom. She wore the ruby vesture. It had been stitched and molded to her comely young body. She fitted it like a marble statue. The train, I noticed, had been put on again, the join hidden with a satin cord. On her head she wore a steeple hat covered in a snowy gauze veil that floated around her bare shoulders, for the robe was cut low, according to the mode.

"Behold my son's new bride," said the old shopkeeper, her crooked skinny face lighting up like the gray aisle of a church in golden sunlight.

We drank the girl's health in wine. I carried home in my basket a cake of vermilion dye the old woman had bought from an Eastern merchant at the door.

I carded a white fleece with wire combs,

as we sat by our fireside at Domremy, the day's work done. I spun a fine slim white thread, even as a spider's spinning. The red dye was bubbling, churning in the vat like a millrace. I dipped the wool and it was red as blood. My arms were dyed scarlet to the shoulder. The courtyard outside was spattered in bloodred drops, as the wool swung to dry on the line. I placed bobbins of red thread in the shuttle, and I wove and wove. When I had enough red weaving, I spread it on the tiles and sheared it to shape. In two days it was finished and I slipped inside my red robe. It was flaring flame color and there was enough red dye over to dye all our household hangings. We redipped all our faded garments. The dye vat remained red forever.

I felt a little shy of my red robe, and did not wear it for the Feast Day of the Saints, as I had intended. But I did wear it. I went to visit Captain de Baudricourt clad in red, as the history books have recorded. I wore it bravely. It gave me hope, as I faced the great soldier and called for men. I felt, maybe, like unto one of the King's daughters of the past, for pride and comeliness.

ne of our few possessions, and most treasured, was an ancient chessboard. The squares were of red and white leather, divided by gold lines. Beneath the board was a box which housed the men. The castle was a crenelated tower, pierced with arrow slits. The knights were exquisitely carved men in armor. But every piece was battered and worn, mended and bound together with wire, so that little of their original beauty remained. Of a winter's evening, some of our neighbors would come in to play. I used to watch the men bending over the board with great intensity and concentration, their eyes fixed on the pieces, their minds calculating the hazards. It was not considered to be a suitable game for young ones. None of us had ever been allowed to play.

My uncle came one evening and was invited to spend the night. Two of the village elders were playing chess, but he bade them continue. He wished to speak with me. I took his riding cloak, drew up his favorite armchair and busied myself unlacing his boots, for he loved to toast his toes before the log fire. As I bent low, struggling with the knotted lace, he whispered in my ear.

"Come back with me, Jeanette my dear, and help me with my market garden. You would find friends in Vaucouleurs and I would give you a happy home. You are lost here in Domremy. They work you as an unpaid servant, and you are like a cooped hen. Would you like to garden for me?"

My heart leaped for joy, because I loved him. I had felt bowed down with the ceaseless toil that was my lot. I could dig almost as strongly as a gardener's boy, and I had a way with plants. It was also the time of my sadness, because my parents had refused to send me to a convent.

"Oh please take me with you," I said, and a boot fell with a thud.

"Good. I will speak with Jacques, and make him release you. You need a change, and I need more help. The arrangement should work very well."

Something suddenly happened, strange and marvelous. An ordinary moment in daily life became a precious flowery moment, like a lily flinging open her petals without warning or sound. The winning player said, "Check." There was a knocking of pieces, and then, "Checkmate to the English king!"

A little carven bishop, one thumb high, hopped off the table and was a man. I saw him in every detail, standing in the shadows, a lovely brown-faced bishop, in tall mitre and embroidered vestments. He held out his gloved hands, and I saw the wound drops of ruby set in the leather. He came to me, held out his arms, and his cloak enveloped me. I heard what he said in my heart.

"Jeanette," he said to me, "you are the Queen of Heaven's pawn. Remember forever the words 'Checkmate to the English king.'"

My parents came in and kindled candles. The fire blazed. The chessmen were put in the box and I had to fetch refreshments and blankets for my uncle, who was sleeping on the settle for the night. The bishop was nowhere to be seen. All was merriment and clacking tongues. We ate by the fireside, drank health to the House of Valois, swore hatred to the English body lice, and spent a good evening.

The guests departed, the younger children went to bed. I could not sleep for excitement. It would be good to stay in Vaucouleurs, the noisy little market town with its taverns ablaze with light, and many churches, the busy market, the fine horses and dogs. Surely my parents would allow me to go for a short visit. Would they? A sudden doubt stabbed me. France and England were at chess, and I was the Queen's pawn.

"Holy Virgin, Mother of God, checkmate young Harry of England before he steals our crown," I said aloud.

I rose from my bed and hurriedly donned my shepherd's cloak. I had to creep silently downstairs on bare feet. I heard my uncle singing to himself by the fireside. He kept late hours. I drew the bolts of the yard door very softly and let myself out as silent as a snake. I had to quiet our watchdog in his kennel, and whisper sweet words to him. He was disappointed to find I was not taking him for a run. I stood in the chill darkness, looking up at the night sky. It was marked with fiery sparks. Tiny gold coins. Counters for the angels' play of chess. I longed for a purse full of star gold to spend on the poor.

I knew then that I had left Domremy. I was no longer there. It was as if I were taking on the part of someone in the religious plays I had seen performed by strolling players. Don a beard, and a young man becomes a Patriarch Noah. Put on a gilded crown of stiffened canvas, and behold God the Father! A little slender boy takes wings and a trumpet, and no one doubts the Herald Angel, for all his disobedience in real home life. Jeanette, the shepherd maid, was somebody from long ago, so old in wisdom and ancient knowledge she was no more the same.

I was a chessman on my square, until God moved me. I was part of a purpose and intent beyond a pawn's knowing. I was caught in a net like a fish, and it was of no avail to leap against the cords that bound me. I must accept the decrees of the Fisher-

man. I understood with deep inward knowing. I was part of a great whole, a spark from
the burning logs, caught in a whirlwind of
tremendous glory. I was like a tiny gold star
in the night sky, being blown by the wonderment of the breath of God.

I shivered slightly and let myself into the
house.

"Who is that?" called my uncle. I entered
the living room.

"Our dog was uneasy. I feared for a robber at the henroost," I said glibly.

"Go to bed, Jeanette dear. Your parents
say they will not let you leave home yet. Do
not worry. I will have another talk with
them. Jacques is so obstinate. Isabeau knows
that I am right."

"Do not *you* worry, uncle," I said, "it is
all arranged."

"Trust a d'Arc for having his own way,
Jeanette! What I say is, Checkmate to the
English king!"

I laughed and went very quietly up to my
room, full of the profound satisfaction that
comes from certainty.

The day came when I was granted audience with de Baudricourt. Through an attendant knight who was his customer, my uncle had made formal request for an interview with the famous captain.

I arrived at the camp, wearing my red robe. I sought admittance, and was greeted rudely by the soldiers. They called me every bad thing a woman has ever been known to be. I was taken to a wooden barracks crowded with soldiers. The floor was piled with equipment, arms and harness from the battlefield that needed sorting and repair. Rainstorms had worked havoc with supply wagons, and sacks of meal were sodden and spoiled. The yard outside was full of vans with broken wheels. Men were busy with hammer and nails. Others bore torn sacks of food to be mended with packthread. Everybody was doing something. The arrival of a peasant girl with a message for the captain was only an annoyance.

I stood my turn in the barrack room, together with other women who had come, each with some complaint and a demand for recompense. There was a gaily colored chart on the wall, pegged with colored flags to show the two armies in position. The sides of the barracks were ranged with ranked lance stands, in which spears stood upright in array, polished bright as silver. There were great piles of rusty breastplates and helmets, iron balls for cannon, corn sieves, bridles, drinking horns, swords and crossbows. Soldiers were on their knees, greasing, sorting, bearing gear out, swiftly, silently, each at his task.

Captain de Baudricourt sat at his desk on a raised dais. He was attending to dispatches. He gave sharp orders and soldiers saluted and hurried away. Others took their places, bearing scrolls to be signed. Some held tiny cipher parchments that had been cunningly wound inside hollow spur shanks, secret and concealed.

De Baudricourt was making a seal. There came a bitter scent of snuffed-out taper, and I watched him pour the scarlet sealing wax from a ladle. As he pressed down the heavy seal, as large as a crown piece, the wax frilled out on the rim, like petals on a crimson rose. He held up the parchment, the blob of seal dangling at the end of the blue lacing, and called for the next complaint. The sergeant at arms stepped forward and said it was a shepherd girl from Domremy. I stood before him.

"And what do you want?" asked the captain wearily. Leaning back in his chair, he looked me over with his red-rimmed ferret eyes. He had had a busy morning with angry women pleading redress for their damaged fields, bitter and sharp-tongued from their wrongs. He was in no mood to hear words of God.

I said, "My Captain, the King of Heaven bids me ask you for an escort. It is God's will that my lord the Dauphin be made King. I must ride to Chinon and speak with him."

"Oh, indeed," said de Baudricourt, in a harsh voice. "This outdoes all requests that ever have been made to me, for barefaced audacity! Do you truly imagine that my soldiers can be spared to ride with you? Do you for a moment think that the Prince would grant an audience to an ignorant shepherd girl?"

"Yes, sire," I said boldly. "Saint Michael tells me that I must strike good blows for France. If you will grant me a horse and men to guard me, the Dauphin *will* hear me."

The captain laughed a hard and grating laugh. "Without doubt the King of Heaven has shown you how to wield arms and lead an army? I am to understand that you know how to ride?"

"Not very well," I said, "but I am able to learn. As it is the will of God, I shall be successful."

The soldiers were listening, gaping. The room was very quiet.

Busying himself with more documents to be signed, the captain asked me a few questions having to do with my revelations and beliefs. They did not truly interest him.

Losing all patience, he looked up coldly.

"I am stronger than your King of Heaven. I will stop you. Go home, shepherdess, and never dare to trouble me again. I will not grant even a safe-conduct on the roads. If my men shame you and pitch you in the ditch, with your throat slit, it will be your own fault, not mine. You are dismissed. Sergeant, turn this woman out!"

I was roughly handled and jostled out of the barracks and thrust through the gate into the open field, with a kick to speed me. Soldiers came striding after me and hustled me out of the camp at a run. The gates were locked behind me. I passed splendid horses, switching flies in the shade, and I felt great despair. I had no thought of mounting a war-horse.

As I drove back to Vaucouleurs with my uncle's friend, I could scarce bear to speak of my humiliation and shame.

I lay wakeful that night in my narrow bed, going over and over the day's events. I heard in my ears the clerks inking their documents with scratchy quills. I heard the clicking spurs, as men stood to attention and saluted. I saw the captain with his red, sunburned neck bulged over the tight neckband of his tunic. In his anger, his enormous, swollen red fist thumped the table. I heard his barking voice, his neighing laugh. He did not believe my words. I had failed my lord, Saint Michael, and was full of self-reproach.

As I lay tossing and turning, I heard a voice. "You must go to de Baudricourt again." My sorrow vanished and my heart filled with joy. In my ears came the sound of a lark's song from a throat that tumbles out tunes, unfettered and free.

I dared, as the history books tell. I went to de Baudricourt again.

I learned later that the captain never believed my visit from Saint Michael was real. He decided that I might be useful. I had seemed to be staunch of purpose, and so single-hearted that the chance was just worth his risking.

I might possibly retrieve the fortunes of France by making men trust in God instead of wallowing in their own despair. I would probably be killed before I reached Chinon. If I did see the Dauphin, assuredly he would judge me a poor demented creature. There was only a chance that he would clutch me as a straw in the wind, an augury of good fortune to drive away his melancholy. The captain knew that his permitting me to go would be seen as madness, but so low had our fortunes fallen that he determined to use me as a spur. I would probably fail and be forgotten. I might goad the obstinate Prince out of his gloomy reflections and force his coronation by the strange perverseness and peculiarity of my absurd claims.

AT COURT

The inn where I stayed for the night before my audience with the Dauphin was crowded and noisy. It was good to have any bed to sleep in, after nights and days in the open, sleeping under haystacks, in barns and finding what cover we could, surrounded by danger. I had seen the fields trampled flat by marching men, bodies left unburied. The cows ate of sour grass and gave poisoned milk. Rats gnawed what little food was left when the soldiers had taken their fill. Dearth and death were everywhere.

I lay in a hard bed betwixt harsh woven sheets. My body ached from hours in the saddle, but I was unable to sleep. The sound of revelers in the parlor below reverberated through the cracks in the floor boards. There

was drunken laughter, screaming and singing that was more like the wail from angry
cats. I could find no rest. I tossed and
turned, thinking of the meeting with the
Dauphin so near at hand.

There was no curtain to the window and
I watched the soft gray dawn streaked with
red. I left my bed and stood breathing the
sweet air at an early hour. A jug of cold
water stood in the corner, with a filthy towel
that I could not use. I rubbed the grime
from my body as best I might, and felt re-
freshed. I sat on the bed to repair my hose.
They had broken into holes in many places.
My heels were raw and blistered, because
the youth's boots I wore were too large for
me. I had a jar of ointment to ease them.

I felt ungainly and ill-clad, in no fit state
to appear at court. The boots were trodden
down and mud-stained, the tunic ill-shaped
and my short cape very unbecoming. I tore
at my tangled hair with my horse comb. I
set on my little round felt cap with the jay
feather clipped in the hem and polished my
belt with my cuff. I plucked a green leaf
from the potted plant at the window, to
wear at my throat. There was noise below.
I could hear shutters creak. Maids sluiced

the cobbles of the yard and farmers arrived with the milk.

I went outside and looked over the stair rail. The guests were mostly farmers who had to leave early for market. They were already eating. I went down and took a place at the table, determined to eat something to keep me steady, for my heart was thundering. I waited impatiently. At last a maid brought me a bowl of curds and steamed grain to stay my hunger.

The farmers stared hard at me, uncertain as to my sex. I heard them muttering. They cast sidelong glances in my direction. Some pushed closer, nudged me and tried to press my leg. One man had a dog with a lame paw. I took it on my lap to examine the injury.

The owner of the dog asked me to drive with him in his cart. I shook my head and said I had work to do. I could find no hurt in the dog's leg, but it liked sitting up to table on my knee.

A plate of egg fry was brought to us, hot, greasy and heavy on the stomach. I asked the slovenly maid to find the dog a bone. The farmers leaned over the table. They could see that I had a way with animals.

Would I look to their horses outside? One had a galled wither, another a running from the eye. Had I any ideas about the horses to race today? I looked into my empty bowl and saw a parti-colored horse gallop past the flag. I told the men what I saw. This caused great excitement and bickering. They shouted and argued. Some said the parti-colored horse had no chance. I paid and made my escape into the stable yard.

There was great activity. Grooms were wisping and hissing, carts were being unladen and horses harnessed. I trembled as if with fever and prayed that my knights, Jean and Bertrand, would soon come to rescue me.

As I was about to hide myself in the saddle room, the dog sniffed me out and disclosed my presence. To my dismay, I saw the men had found me.

"One moment, young master," said one. "I have more what you might call a gnaw, if you understand me. Comes on at night, right under my belly band. A nag-gnaw, not a needle-nag, jumpy-up-and-down-like. My wife says it's only the wind, from too much fatty pork, but what should I take for it?"

"Here is my little nag with the weepy humors," said another. "Every time she hears a huntsman sound his horn, she brings out a shiver and begins to sweat. Ought I to cut her bean feed down?"

"I'd say that this mare had the warble fly on the shoulder. She should not wear the collar," said a third. "But why say you a motley horse will win? Me, I have put my money on the royal black."

I laid salve to the warbled wither, I gave advice.

Then the arrival of two court guards in the stable yard filled me with terror. They carried tall pikes and had come to lead me to the castle.

There was a cold and deathly silence in the courtyard. Grooms gawped and stared with wide eyes. The farmers were speechless. They thought that I was being led to execution for some crime.

Sick with fear, I was marched away between the guards. What awaited me? Why had I come away from my home? I had forgotten every word I had so carefully prepared to speak. I was taken over the drawbridge, through the castle door and was set to wait in a small antechamber. I was very alone. There was no Saint, no Voice, only my hurried breathing, the pulse of my heart. I had a needle-nag too, to keep me company, or maybe it was more of a gnaw.

I waited and waited and waited, in the little stone room. At last the door opened and an ugly man came in. He had a nose like a swan's beak, as purple as the long velvet robe that reached to the top of his pointed shoes. He had a rich gold chain dangling and fashionable hanging sleeves, open at the shoulder to reveal an inner tunic of blue satin with tight wristbands. His head was swathed in velvet with a trailing end that touched his shoulder.

He stared rudely and I met his gaze. I stood stiff, squared my shoulders and looked into his goose face unflinchingly.

"You are the swineherd from Lorraine, are you not?" he said sourly.

"I am Jeanette of the d'Arcs of Domremy," I said.

He led me round and round the winding stairway, up and up and up. Then he flung open a door, gripped my arm, and swung me into a crowded room. High-pitched chatter ceased and curious eyes turned on me.

"Your Royal Highness, the goosegirl," said the chamberlain.

I was in a vaulted chamber ablaze with light. It was crowded with women in robes as bright as spring flowers, and men like gay butterflies. The scene glowed like a jewel with colors. The whole room was like a window of rare baked glass. The floor was thick with mossy carpet. The walls were studded with golden-framed pictures. The furniture was gold, cushioned in blue velvet.

The chamberlain prodded me through the twittering crowd toward a man seated in a wide gold chair, placed on a raised dais.

"Kneel to his highness, Prince Charles," whispered the chamberlain.

I hesitated. I was uneasy. The man's face was dark. He held out jeweled fingers for me to kiss, but I could not. This was no prince, my heart told me.

I followed the gaze of the hounds that clustered around the feet of a pale man clad in gray. He stood apart.

He was their master and mine. I knew, I knew. Had I not seen his face in a painting? I looked and over his head I saw a point of light. I tore free from the chamberlain and flung myself at the feet of the man in gray.

"He is the one you seek," he said, pointing to the man on the dais.

I threw back the hood of my cape and doffed my cap.

"Are you not my lord, Prince Charles, to be made King of France?"

"How are you so sure?" questioned the gray man.

"You have tried to trick me, Sire, but I see the Crown. I see the gold Crown above you. There. There. Can you not feel it?"

"I will speak with you alone." The gray man who spoke was my Prince, the rightful King.

The chamberlain escorted me out through the throng of knights, courtiers and twittery ladies of the court. I found myself in a room lined with racks of parchment. There was a chair of state for the Dauphin and a stool for me to sit on. A scribe came to make record of the audience with my Prince.

The Dauphin came into the room. Courtiers bowed him to his seat and withdrew. "Tell me your message and be brief," said the Prince.

"I come from the King of Heaven for your Crowning," I said.

Thus began the strange alliance that wove me into his tapestry.

oments and figures from the life I spent at court before the Coronation come alive before my eyes.

The castle in which the Dauphin was living at Chinon was set in fair green meads. I was given a room shaped with eight sides. It overlooked the park. It was simply furnished, with an oaken armor press, and a tall curtained bed. Candle holders lance-high stood to either side of the fireplace, and on the walls hung paintings of the ancient kings of France.

The Dauphin was a weak likeable man, prone to moods of great sadness. He was a strange, ugly creature, with a shaven poll, thin lips and jutting ears. His eyes were weak and fringed with pale lashes. His complexion was sallow, marked with smallpox. His teeth were big, like horse teeth. He had bandy legs and great knobbly knock-knees.

The Dauphin was loveable in his way and I became very fond of him. For a time, he trusted me with all his secrets.

He was ever seeking to learn the future from any vagrant tinker or man of dreams. He was very superstitious, trying to learn the future by astrology, soothsaying, fortune-telling, by dice and many other means.

He found in me something new and stimulating because of my strange gifts. He hoped to read his destiny from my lips, but when it was revealed, he strove against it.

One of the reasons for my success at court was my skill as a healer. The Dauphin was sickly but his discomforts were all brought on by his overeating, and by his rarely being in the fresh air. I told him he must control his indulgence in fine fare. He must be more active.

The result of his acting on my advice soon showed itself in his whole demeanor, and in the brightness of his eyes. The royal physician was jealous of me and spread ill-natured tales to disgrace me. He knew the right

95

remedies for sickness. My knowledge was worthless. He had studied medicine in the University of Padua, and was skilled in every branch of the art.

The Dauphin ruled the court with skill. He liked order and beauty. He took an interest in every department, from kitchen to armory, from stables to tilting ground.

Provisions for the court table were supplied by the Dauphin's own farms. Wains laden with eggs, butter, game and fish arrived each day, and the Prince liked the best that could be obtained and gave of his best to all at his court.

He greatly enjoyed dancing and displays of tilting held in the castle grounds. Even when war had impoverished his coffer, still did he entertain his friends with lavish generosity. He was good company in his way, clever at making jests and telling stories.

The lords and ladies amongst whom I mixed tolerated me as a new thing. They regarded me rather in the way they might a court jester. So long as I remained in favor my opinion was of value, and I was never sneered at.

I was made to wear a woman's robe when dining at the royal table. The royal housekeeper was a kind, motherly woman. A robe belonging to a court lady had been given to her and we stitched it to fit me. It was lime-leaf green and had puckered sleeves that tapered to a point over my wrists. The low-cut collar showed much of my neck and shoulders. The skirts irked me and the steeple hat chafed my head.

The ladies-in-waiting wanted me to reduce my sunburn with starch paste. The fashion was for very white skin, hair shaved back from the forehead, arched and blackened brows. I refused to blanch my skin. It was sound and healthy, tinted with natural color. I pulled a few hairs from my brows. This was the limit of my beautifying—this and the trimming of my lustrous hair, which grew very rapidly.

The court ladies were spoiled and silly. I heartily disliked them. They gossiped and giggled and told tales and encouraged the Dauphin in his weakness. They were like flowers cultured in a hothouse that wither and droop at the first puff of fresh air. They were in every way different from the women of Domremy. The village women had no time to restrict their bodies with lacings, or to embroider pictures. They had to work half the night to keep their children from starving. They loved God and found Heaven whilst the court ladies, I was ashamed to learn, often embraced lovers and wandered far from virtue.

I longed to escape from the rigid rules of court life that I was never bred for.

There was a little nervous whippet, that was specially fond of me. I felt that there was a kinship between us. She was a creature of infinite grace, but she had no freedom. She was kenneled and chained and rarely allowed to romp on the greensward.

One day I set her free. I went down the winding castle stairs with the whippet bounding by my side. I took her out to the tiltyard for a frolic.

For a moment I had broken the leash that held me. I saw the clouds piling up, pushed by an invisible power. Trees bent before the wind's breath. As I ran with the dog, I was young and pliant as a larch sapling, but an earthbound creature, I could not enjoy the freedom of the air like birds. I heard the striking of the bell, calling the courtiers to the evening meal. I stayed outside, gamboling with the whippet.

From childhood I had lived close to nature, but almost always too hard-worked for lingering and marveling at wonders all around me. Now, as I ran in the park, I felt that I was a part of it. I shared its sap and movement. I felt the wild rush of beating wings, the slow rise of life in awakening trees, the thrust of grass-blades, as clay melted after the grip of frost. I was no longer a woman walking on dead earth, curry-combed and prodded by the gardeners like a horse's coat. I was Nature, warmed and thrilled by her tides. I was better than the flowers, but not so beautiful. I was stronger than the tree, for it obeyed a law it might not change. It had to suffer the gash of the woodman's ax. The stream that chuckled and frothed was kept in bounds against its will and made to run in a fixed groove.

I was a part of nature, but far more rich and fortunate than those other parts. No gardener might mow me down with a scythe, no farmer chop at me. Indeed, I was

99

wounded daily, but the hurt reached only a small part of me. If I lay slain, in a pool of blood with no breath in me, I would not be a felled tree.

I was a part of something that went on. No sword any longer held any terror for me.

What I have put in words here was something I could never have described at the time. I came back to myself, the bodily part, full of defect and failing, but there was a change in me.

I was no longer only nature's green thing, but a thing the King of Heaven made use of. I blossomed and bore fruit for Him alone. I was an everlasting joy, housed in body, full of sap and soundness and good bone. God had lifted me higher than the whippet that bounded with life's urge. My heart had become God's cup.

I returned to the castle, to take my share of the good things given, to joke and laugh, but I was no longer a member of the court.

very day I rode in the green meadows of Chinon. There was always something for me to do. My days were never fruitless. I learned to tilt and drive a pointed stave into a sack as I passed at full gallop. We had many exercises to test horsemanship, so that I soon became something of an expert in the saddle.

I remember one day I was sitting in the saddle room after exercise, rubbing tallow into cracked leather. The stable boys were busy going over the harness and polishing bit cups. I tried to see that they kept the gear in good repair. The room was heated to a stifling heat by a charcoal brazier and the saddles were stacked on racks in front to dry sweat from the linings.

I had been listening to the chatter around me and I had an idea. The boys said the country had no faith in the French crown. It would be best, they thought, to make a peace with the English. They were established in vast strength and there was no hope.

I knew what I must do. I said there *was* hope! The tide had set in our favor and we must raise to glory the Royal House of Valois. We must start our campaign by changing the horse trappings, making them bright and bold.

The stable boys growled and grumbled, saying it would cost money and there was none to spare. I said I would get sewing maids to repair the horse covers. The lilies could be whitened, the stars regilded, and the bridles hung with ribbon favors. I would have the horses' manes and tails plaited with bright cords.

The boys showed interest and seemed cheered. They said there was a trunk full of horse trappings that maybe had not rotted through with age and disuse. I had them fling it down from the loft, and with great difficulty we prized open the creaking lid. Inside were ancient horsecloths, somewhat nibbled by the moth, but not unusable. There were metal frontlets to sew on the horse bands for warding off the Evil Eye. I had them laid out on the floor to examine in detail. We rubbed off the grime and mildew, and wiped them with oil until they shone with brightness. We spread the horse coverings over boards and pressed them with heavy hot irons, so that they steamed and lost their wrinkles.

I gathered together a bevy of serving maids. We laundered and stitched back the fringes, and mended the armorial bearings that hung upon the chest bands and cruppers. The moth holes were patched and the raw edges whipped with colored cord.

At the end of some days we had made a brave array. We had a parade of the royal stud clad in their finery. The manes were oiled and coiled into little tight ringlets and tied with ribbon. Tails were plaited and bunched. Our horses were the pride of the countryside, beautifully groomed and brightly caparisoned.

We petitioned the Dauphin that he visit the stables. He was delighted at the sight. He praised his grooms for their industry and I let them take credit for all that I had done.

There was another change. Some of the grooms had been accustomed to gamble and use foul language, but in my presence they refrained and behaved decently. Even the gloomiest stable boy was disposed to be friendly.

My idea had changed wondrously all those gloomy men. All worked with cheerfulness and pride as for a mighty king. When word came to them that the Prince was to be crowned, a wave of loyalty broke over them and they vowed to give their lives in his cause.

he Dauphin had a passion for curios, and prized his collection of little treasures brought from far-off lands. I will tell of one episode having to do with one of these, a favorite figure that I now know represented Buddha.

The Dauphin had in his cabinet a figure carved from green stone. It was a half-naked man, with his hair done up in a strange knot, legs folded, his eyes closed in prayer. The Dauphin told me the man was venerated as a god in the East.

I was attracted to the figure. I did not feel that it was evil, but rather that it belonged to another world, remote from mine. It had a strange fascination for me and my eyes were drawn to the little green man as he sat on the shelf in the Dauphin's cabinet.

One day, as the Dauphin was examining his treasures, I asked if I might hold the figure in my hands. He agreed and I sat on his tall gilded chair, with the little man before me. The Dauphin asked me what I could see. I *did* begin to see things at once. Scenes passed before my eyes and I felt tempted to drop the image, and yet was unable to cease from seeing. There was watery green-and-crested coiling water, veined, variegated, pure and unmuddied green, like the figure before me. A boat was plowing the waves, men bearing hard on heavy oars. There was a man with gold bands around his naked arms, tall and handsome with black curling hair.

The boat was nearing the shore and it grated on the shingle. The men waded to the beach, dragged up the boat behind them and made it fast. It was a sun-scorched land, with trees like fern leaves, unlike any that I had ever seen. The picture faded and another came before my eyes.

I saw a big hall, high-roofed and curiously painted. At one end was a platform, and on it I saw my green man, but tall, with the piled-up topknot of hair. He was larger than life, and carved of the same pale translucent green stone that faded to creamy white. There were bowls of incense before him and I saw the smoke twining upward like skeined wool. Short, swarthy men clad in white were bowing before the image.

A curtain at the end of the hall parted, and the captain from overseas with the gold armlets strode in. He began to make some proposition to the men, which they refused. There seemed to be a headman, a kind of priest. I saw him distinctly, shaking his head and taking up his stand in front of the image. I felt myself *pulled*, as though by some irresistible force, and made to join the white robed men in their foreign temple, for so, by inspiration, I knew it to be. They were in danger of losing a precious treasure. The captain was a robber.

I began to tremble, and I said that there was evil ahead, robbery and violence. The captain drew his sword and the scene dimmed.

My vision was shattered, for a chamberlain came in. Bowing low, he said a foreign merchant craved an audience. The man had a bundle of treasures, going very cheap, that the Prince would surely value. The Dauphin never could resist buying curios from abroad. Now I felt very anxious, for he had no money to spare on such trifles. He had the merchant brought to him. The man came in, and I started. Looking in his face, I recognized the bronze-skinned man whom I had just seen. He was the headman, the priest, clad in a different guise.

The Eastern merchant unrolled his bundle and spread beautiful embroideries upon the floor. He looked at me hard and came to my side, saying, "Mademoiselle, that green figure is worth much money. He belongs in the country from which I come. He wants to go home. He does not belong here. I shall take him home with me. I can pay good money."

The Dauphin was astonished. He had not thought it a costly piece. He considered it to be only a curio from a far land, rather prettily carved. He said sharply that he was not accustomed to be asked such favors. Most of his treasures had belonged to his ancestors and he valued them highly. As it

108

was wartime, he *had* parted with some of his jewels. This was a calamity much to be regretted. The green man was not for sale.

The merchant said he lived by selling things from place to place. He had little to offer, but his friends would give a goodly sum if only he might have the image. He would return in a few months and pay for it. The Dauphin said that if he could pay highly in coins of the realm, the idol was possibly for sale. He did not hold for it a *special* love, as he did for various other trinkets in his cabinet.

The merchant asked a favor. Might he hold the image in his hands? Before the Dauphin could answer, the man took the figure from my lap and a strange thing happened. The air seemed filled with a smell of incense so sweet and powerful that my head reeled.

The merchant smiled and put the green man back within the open cabinet. I saw him do it. I looked at the little figure smiling serenely, with closed eyes, in deep meditation as he squatted on the shelf. I closed the door of the cabinet, turned the key, and handed it back to the Dauphin.

After a short time the merchant rolled up his belongings, having left with us a few inexpensive articles. He bowed and placed both hands on his brow, saying most politely that he hoped the Prince would be crowned King. Then he left.

The Dauphin unlocked his cabinet and put in his newly acquired treasures. He had purchased some small boxes studded with stones and inlaid with shell, some rings of cheap metal, and a string of amber.

Suddenly he gave a cry. The little green man was no longer there! I was amazed. I had seen him myself. I knew that I could not be mistaken, but we searched in vain.

That night I had a strange dream. The image became alive and came to me. I saw a wise man with long earlobes and a most benign face. He said he was a teacher of the truth. Men called him Buddha! He had taken on life in a far land and had come to *me*, because the spirit of truth was in me. I was not to worry because the image had disappeared.

I wakened, feeling very much consoled but not entirely satisfied. I felt the Dauphin suspected me of having taken the figure. How *could* it have disappeared? I prayed, but could get no clear guidance.

The matter was hushed up, but some months later the merchant returned. He brought to the Dauphin a bag containing gold pieces. He could now pay.

The Dauphin said sadly that the idol was missing. The merchant gave a radiant smile, showing marvelous white teeth. He said his master had informed him of the fact, and had saved him the trouble of conveying the treasure back to its resting place within the temple. It was an image of the Holy Buddha and by magic it had been taken home.

That was the end of the episode. The Dauphin gladly accepted the money, but how the image had been stolen remained a mystery.

Thinking over what had taken place, I felt certain that a spell had been laid upon me when the fumes of incense made my head spin. The merchant had never returned the image to the cabinet. By willpower he had implanted this impression in my mind when the little green man was safely hidden in the robes of his dress.

Who was the captain who had stolen the image? I never learned his name. I did find out that one of the Dauphin's ancestors had visited an Eastern island by boat many centuries before.

The Dauphin had an insatiable desire to know the future. He visited the strangest seers and prophets, fortune-tellers and palmists. They gave conflicting prophecies, no one of which was the perfect truth. One day he called for me in the audience chamber. He told me that we were to visit the home of a nobleman nearby who had amazing gifts of divination. His friend, he said, had been taught to read the future by a man from a foreign land beyond the seas.

The Dauphin's dreams had depressed him. He thought the battle reports were bad. He was filled with premonitions of evil. The moon was in decline, opposed by trouble-making stars. His country was burned barren to the very bones by bitter war.

We visited the great lord. His home was filled with woven tapestries and gold-rimmed paintings, rich carpets and polished wood. I saw pictures of the kings and queens of France whom I had learned to distinguish by name.

The Dauphin was seated in the place of honor. The nobleman with his friends stood respectfully around him, as was the custom. They began a heated discussion of military tactics and I was left out of it all, free to find joy in the beauty around me.

The vaulted ceiling was painted blue like the sky, and was besprinkled with little gold stars. At the four corners of the room were child angels, rosy and plump, playing pipes and blowing out their bowed red lips.

One of the retainers spoke to me. "I have heard stories about you, mademoiselle. Men say the Prince will receive his crown before he reaches thirty. I cannot believe that. The English king will be too strong for him." He whispered in my ear. "The blood royal comes from tainted stock!"

The Dauphin had finished speaking and he signed to me to stand before him. Our host was about to read the future.

He took from a recess a heavy gold goblet covered with cloth. He held the goblet aloft, chanting words in a foreign tongue. Then he emptied out the contents of the cup on a little round table marked in squares. It was a strange assortment of objects that came rolling—a gold ring, a coin, a lump of crystal, a key, a cross of wood and a stick of charcoal. The lord studied the position of each object and made his prediction.

"Rain gushing, rain to swell the rivers and wash away the pontoon bridges."

The gold ring had fallen off the rim of the table. This was a bad omen, for it meant broken marriage. The tiny wooden cross was in the center underneath the stick of charcoal.

"Death and destruction to the English, and certain disaster for their king's men . . . unless . . ."

The lord continued. Having raised the Dauphin's hopes, he dashed them to the ground. He had come upon the key to the situation, he said, but first, before fortune could change, he must be made General-in-Command. He spoke vehemently, watching the Dauphin's face.

His words were meaningless and false! I begged to be allowed to speak. The Dauphin said in apology that I was his little shepherdess counselor, who said clever things in her simple way. If his host permitted, I might be allowed to say my bit.

"What did the cross and the charcoal mean?" asked the Dauphin, pointing to the center of the table.

The lord was much displeased. He did not like a rival prophet to interfere with his predictions. He was clearly afraid lest I weaken the impression he had made.

I stepped forward to face the Dauphin's chair. Between us was the gaming table.

"God gives me to say that by the gold coin in ascendant above the cross, I see you are the chosen King of France."

I felt inspired. I told him many things about to be.

The lord's face was dark and sullen, and he broke in angrily. He said he did not know what sort of woman I might be, but it was an impertinence for me to prophesy. I was a bad counselor, and completely untrustworthy. He hoped the Dauphin would have me silenced and removed from his presence.

The Dauphin hesitated, looking first at me and then at his host. He signed for me to withdraw. As I was about to leave the room, my arms held by two attendants, I spoke once more.

"Our fortunes will grow and grow, like the swollen rivers. We will find the means to drive out the enemies of France. The stars are on our side! We want men and arms and horses and gold, and more men, and more arms, and the power of the Great God within us!"

I was dragged away and bundled into a cart, and driven back to Chinon. There I was taken to my room and locked in.

I sat on my bed and worked at repairing the sheath of my dagger until the room grew too dark for me to see.

There came a knock, and the chamberlain opened the door. He was my bitter enemy who had done me much hurt. He ordered me to follow him at once to the Dauphin's private chapel.

I entered the small dim room lighted by myriad winking tapers, where the Dauphin each day heard Mass. He rose from his knees before the altar and came toward me.

I saw by his swollen eyes that he had been weeping.

"My shepherdess," he said gently, "I am the rightful King of France who must wear the crown of his ancestors. My mind is resolute."

He held out his fingers for me to kiss, and I prayed beside him far into the night.

I had deciphered the signs on the board. I knew the crystal signified truth, clear vision and purity; the key, the means to be employed. The iron nail signified armor and cannon. The noble lord had said so himself. The lump of chalk was a symbol of documents and dispatches, orders given.

I had seen in my head the forts and castles, armies in disarray, towers falling before the cannon's fiery breath. I could have read the Dauphin's future without the goblet.

The little wooden cross puzzled me, and the stick of charred wood. Fire and destruction in the fair fields of France, most like, and the cross was the standard of the King of Heaven.

efore his Coronation, I spoke to the Dauphin without fear. God gave me courage. I said, "Sire, I have a message for you. Take heed that you do not become filled with pride at the rising of your star, the crowning in state that is being prepared. Do not think only of your robe of silver tissue, the rubies in your crown, crowds hailing you on bended knees, heralds, and royal banners straining at their poles. Be humble at the moment of your triumph and God will make of you a wise ruler."

The Dauphin was silent. He seemed impressed by my words. He searched my face and read such firm conviction that God had spoken through me, that he could not answer angrily. Taking me by the hand, he led.

me through the garden to a little hothouse lined with lead pipes over charcoal braziers. There rare plants and sweet herbs were reared for the palace. Rows of fragrant plants were ranged in pots on the slatted shelves.

The Dauphin said, "Shepherdess, I could have you whipped through the streets at the cart's tail for your audacity. I could have your nose slit and your ears cropped. Many have suffered this for less than you have spoken. I will not punish you, as a sign that I have a God and a conscience. Make me a crown of that climbing plant. I will wear it before God, His humble servant."

I saw a pair of shears hanging from a peg. With these I chopped sprays of the sweet-scented flowery plant with tiny leaves. I twined and twisted them to form a circlet and added some bright blossoms for gems, securing them with strands of dried grass. I lifted the wreath and placed it over the velvet cap he wore when walking. A trailer of velvet hung over one shoulder according to fashion. The Dauphin laughed as happily as a child. I bowed to him and sank on one knee. In a sudden impulse he snapped off a

curling green-veined lily as stiff as satin parchment, and put it in my hand for scepter.

I said, "All hail, Charles, seventh of the name. Blessed be thou amongst monarchs!"

The Dauphin said, "O God, make of me a good king. I wear this crown as a token of my wish to be humble. Keep me lowly and meek of heart like Jesus."

We heard the baying of the hounds, and I rose hurriedly from my knees, knowing that we were about to be discovered.

The Dauphin tore off his garland, flung it over my head, and began to brush white petals and golden dust from his tunic.

Courtiers were seeking him, with the dogs on leash. The whippet bounded forward to eel in and out around his legs and leap and love him, tremulous with joy.

"My lord, we have been seeking you everywhere. Your presence is urgently desired within the audience chamber," said a courtier, bowing low.

The Dauphin hurried away, the hounds barking and baying like a clamor of harsh bells.

I was alone and forgotten. I hung the

120

wreath on the little stone god of love by the fish pool.

The gardener was approaching, followed by the garden boy wheeling a barrow. The gardener scowled at me.

"You, mademoiselle! What do you do with one of my lilies? You dare to go plucking the royal lilies to decorate a heathen statue! It is a true disgrace in a Christian land! I shall make a report of it to the chamberlain. Our Prince is specially particular over his lilies."

I knew that I was in for trouble, but the whippet had come back to fetch me. She was on her hind legs, pawing the little sack at my waist. She had been taught to fetch and carry.

I placed the lily gently between her thin jaws and sent her racing after her lord.

The Dauphin held a most splendid reception before his Coronation.

I helped the head gardener and chamberlain to fill the hall of welcome with flowers. We placed basins of fern and blossom, hung swaying garlands of gilded leaves and gay ribbons. Little stone love gods holding horns filled with Eastern scents were in the corners of the room. The Dauphin poured costly scent upon the moss although the flaring lilies made one swoon with the sweetness of their own breath.

The court dogs had their nails clipped and their silky coats brushed, combed and oiled. They wore pale blue rosettes in their collars—the Dauphin's favorite color.

For the feast, the pastrycooks had outdone themselves in molding delicate pastries into fanciful shapes. When the guests had their fill of these delicacies, they took seats to watch an entertainment.

The Dauphin had taught some of his tame birds to do tricks. He had a curious bird bought from a sailor. Its plumage was emerald and blue, its beak like a goldsmith's pincers. It was tethered by a chain on its leg. Sidling up the Dauphin's arm, its head cocked sideways, it would say, "Charles of Valois!" in a harsh grating voice. Then it would snap up a nut from his Liege Lord's fingers.

I had taught the hounds to balance on their hind legs and beg for cake. From a cage held by two pages, came tame doves that alighted on our heads and took cherries from between our lips. We gave them poems written on scraps of parchment, whereupon each dove flew to a gaudily attired lady, and dropped the poem in her lap.

One courtier had a little enamel green snake that coiled inside his doublet. It would strike out its funny little flat head to flick a forked tongue, and then wriggle back

123

again. There was a tame swan that swayed in, like a boat coming ashore. It shoveled corn with its heavy knobbed beak, hooped up its writhing neck and hissed. Then the courtier led it out again.

I was given a small orange-haired monkey to fondle. It had a little old-woman face, covered in hairless kid, and round black unwinking eyes. It bit me sharply and I gave a shrill squeal.

Wine flowed, pipers piped, harps twanged, bells chimed, boys sang. A bronze-skinned girl, partly clad in swirling gauzy veils, was doing a dance, as supple as a flower in the wind. She swung a leg ringed round in bangles, and doubled backward in a wheel throw like an acrobat at the fair. There was a crackle of clapping hands.

I enjoyed the merry tales of the guests. As best I could I tried to conduct myself worthily before these great lords in cut velvet tunics, and ladies sparkling with gems and glowing in satin and silver tissue.

A log fell with a crash of golden rain from the crackling fire kindled to warm the revelers. Blazing soot clung to the blackened chimney like stars in a midnight sky. Laugh-

ter and music faded far away, and I was lost
in a world of vision.

I saw battle, spurting flame, and tumbling
towers, dying men. I saw our army felled
before Paris because of his delay. I saw retreat, humiliation, loss of fame. I looked to
the Dauphin, who sat ahead of me, watching the dancing girl.

For the second time, over his head I saw
the Crown. It was fretted like a tower of
filigree gold, set with burning stones. It was
the most beautiful crown that ever one
could seek. My heart thrilled to the sight of
it. The rubies were red as blood, the pearls
gleamed. Diamonds and emeralds seemed
to softly melt, then turn solid again to flash
fire. Over the Crown were rays from the
Dove of the Spirit, formed in white light.

It was the Crown of France. Every doubt
vanished as I beheld it.

The dancing had stopped, and the guests
had winecups in their hands to drink the
health of Charles, their future King. Hardly
had they lowered their goblets, when a
chamberlain entered the room. Grave-faced,
he bent over the Dauphin and whispered to
him. As the guests took their places at the

gaming tables to play at cards, the Dauphin beckoned me to his side. His face was very white and he was much disturbed.

"Shepherdess," he said, "my spies bring bad news. Paris has been reinforced against us."

"God bids me say that you must be crowned and with all speed attack Paris!" I answered boldly. The words flowed together like the gems in his crown.

"What do you see over my head that you stare so?" he asked.

"The Crown of France, glorified and made perfect. There will come a time when there is no king, a time when a glorious one will restore France. A man full of wisdom and virtue."

The Dauphin laughed. "Shepherdess, you are talking folly. I may fail, but there will never be a time without a king. The people worship and adore our Royal House."

"Charles of Valois! Charles of Valois!" cackled the brightly colored bird. The guests took up the cry as more wine brimmed their goblets.

"Long live our future King, Charles the Seventh of France," they cried as one man.

hen my Liege Lord came to be crowned, heralds went forth, blazing the news abroad. They were clad in heraldic tunics stiff with gold and silver leaf on silk cloth, and the armorial arms blazoned in jewel-bright hues. They blew thin silver trumpets summoning all loyal patriots to prepare with prayer and fasting, that the doom and destruction which lay upon France might be lifted.

The Prince held service in his private chapel, and wore a shirt of rough hair next to his flesh. He became sober and pious, and gave up jousting, dancing, games of chance.

The court was swept, the tapestry darned, the cushions stuffed. The robes of the waiting women were dipped in dyes, and their veilings freshly laundered. The grime of years was mopped away and the paintwork scoured to a sparkle.

The Cathedral of Rheims was burnished bright. Every shield was washed and licked with new color. The cathedral was carpeted in rose carmine. A gilded chair was placed at the High Altar for the King.

Charles wished me to be made beautiful, as his companion and fortune bringer. I was measured for new garments. I grew weary of standing, as the court robe maker fitted velvet to my figure and stuck me with sharp pins. The loveliest sky-blue velvet, pansy-petal soft, was formed as a doublet ending on my hips. A short cloak was lined with rich satin, white like curdled cream. I stroked it lovingly, like the cat I had when I was a child. My hair was frizzed into tight curls with burning-hot irons that scorched my cheek.

The Coronation was the most glorious day of my life.

I stood ready, beautifully clad for the ceremony, in the sky-blue velvet, with a heron's feather around my cap. The short cloak hung to my waist. I bore aloft the royal standard, the Lilies of France.

For one brief instant, I forgot the pain and wounds of France, which were so constantly before me.

The court was clad in all the colors of the rainbow. Every knight and lady wore gold and silver tissue, and damask silk.

The Prince was carried on a litter. The Archbishop wore a cape stiff with dust of diamonds and gold thread. In the procession were trumpeters with silver trumpets, priests bearing tall candles, trainbearers, ladies-in-waiting, officers of the household. Boys sang like young angels, and pages scattered rose leaves. Women shed tears and Charles himself was overcome with emotion.

I felt sad, in the midst of so much glory and majesty, thinking of the torrents of blood men had shed, that France might have her king.

hen I was Jeanette d'Arc, a child at Domremy, we used to celebrate the feast of May according to ancient custom. We bent willow wands to form a hoop, and twined them with garlands. We made a doll of straw decorated with blossoms surrounded with ferns, to swing aloft as May's Queen. We would then go from house to house, begging for cakes, and singing songs to celebrate the first of May. We took great pains to bedeck worthily our fair Queen of the May. In our eyes she was beauteous and much beloved.

It was May Day and my country was at war. I had become a soldier on campaign. So great were the terrible desolation and dearth, that few of the lords and ladies could have spared even a small coin for the ragged children in their Maying.

I was riding to war. It was around me, in all its ugly horror, and I had no time for such foolery. I trotted through a hamlet, with my escort of knights, and in the green lane I was set on by a mob of little dirty children, holding aloft a bower of leaves tied between two poles.

"Spare a gift for our lady of Spring. Give us a piece of silver, Monsieur Soldier. Lovely May Queen to bring you fortune. We have no money to buy bread."

They were all around my horse. I had to rein abruptly for fear of trampling them as they clamored for alms.

My horse bickered sideways and I could scarce control him. When they heard my voice and knew that I was a woman, they pressed in on me and held up the queen for me to kiss. She was a billet of wood. Her eyes were two holes burned with hot wire. A tuft of sheep wool was nailed to her poll for hair, and a blob of red sheep raddle made a mouth. She was wound in a filthy rag of lace.

133

She swung crazily head down, and my horse snatched playfully at the wilted gilly-flowers that formed her bower. This caused a storm of fury. I had spoiled their queen and must pay for the damage. The children screamed and wailed and beat my armored foot with their fists. My knights told them to be gone, and drew their swords, but I had an idea.

"Pluck me some fresh flowers and I will mend the canopy. We will all go a-Maying together," I said to the children. They raced away, and a few moments later returned, hot and panting, having pillaged a hayfield. I bit off some lengths of packthread from a spool I carried, and we fashioned garlands. My bridle and bit cups were adorned with daisy and clover sprays. My saddlecloth was powdered in yellow gold dust, fallen buttercup's gilding. Even my spurs were tied with the little bright blossoms of the grass, and I had ferns on my helm. I tied the queen aloft, hung about with chained daisies. Then we went forward, with my children marching in rank behind us, to beg money for bread.

Presently we came to a country mansion.

Its drive was untended, the grass of the bowling green rank and unrolled. The trees were ivy-grown and burdened with dead wood. I clattered down the drive, with my escort complaining and begging me to turn back. It was unfitting for a captain to behave as I was doing. I did not heed but rode up to the heavy iron-knobbed door and lifted the knocker ring with my sword tip. It clanged like a church bell. Then there was heavy silence. I waited and my army of children rushed up to join me and stood to attention.

The door opened creakily. A bent old manservant, with a hairy goat face, clad in rusty faded livery, looked out at us.

"Go away," he said gruffly. "My lady cannot house soldiers, and we have no fodder or grazing. We have nothing to give. Our last bed sheet has gone for wound covering. We have not enough for ourselves."

"I crave alms for hungry children. You cannot refuse to give for the May Queen," I said, and held out my plumed helm for a begging bowl. The servant blinked and twittered, pointing to the round hoof dents on the turf behind us, and the drooping bushes the children had robbed in passing. He tried to close the door, but the two older children holding the poles of the May Queen dodged behind him and pushed inside the house. He was surrounded by children. He swore he would set the dog on us, to tear us to tatters, but he was unable to drive us away. We were too many for him.

Voices came from inside the house and the great lady appeared. She wore a robe of brocade, sadly in need of repair. A workwoman's apron was tied at her waist. Her face was thin and blue-shadowed from weariness and lack of food.

"Why has my house been invaded in this unmannerly fashion?" she said to me. "I cannot spare money for beggars. I have had soldiers billeted in my hall. They robbed me and did great hurt. We have nothing left. The war has taken all. My husband has been killed and my child died of tainted food. We are ruined."

"This is May Day," I said, as I saw the children holding up the doll for her to admire. "There is something left that you can give. For the sake of the child you have lost, I call for alms. Alms in the name of the

Queen of Heaven, for our lady of Spring."

"No, no, go away, you dirty rough children. Drive them away, Philippe. Hit them with your staff. The last egg has been filched from us, our cows were driven off, the horses are gone. We have no hams hidden up the chimney and the meal box is empty. The mice are better fed. Go away, you armed trollop. Whoever you are, go with your gang of thieves. You are worse than the plague that kills the swine."

She began to weep. I dismounted and sank on my knees before her.

"I crave alms, madame, alms in God's name. Give something."

My manner moved her and she turned back into the house. I told my children to sing a May melody.

The lady returned with a doll in her hands, its waxen face crowned in curls. It had a velvet robe of blue, sparkling in beads, and little soft waggly arms. Truly the queen of dolls, the most beauteous doll I had ever set eyes on.

"Here is a queen for you. Perchance she will turn your fortunes. Go away, for I can bear no more," said the lady. The children were hooping her around with their thin arms, and kissing her toil-roughened hands. Philippe flung away the wood stump and fixed the doll in its place, screwing up his wattled old face to give a sour kiss.

As I led my horse down the drive, we sang and sang in as many tones as a chime of bells. A sudden impulse made me return back, pick up the stump of wood, and tie her to the cantle of my saddle. I trod out the hoofprints as best I could, and remounted at the gate. The children were showing their doll to a farmer in a cart.

I waved farewell and trotted away in great heart. From a wild cherry, dripping dappled snow blossoms, I plucked some sprays and made a fresh bower for my wooden May Queen. I begged a little money from the wayfarers I met on the road, and sent a knight galloping back to give to the children. It was a royal May Day, blest by the Queen whom all men should honor, the blessed Mary, Queen of Heaven.

When we reached camp, my men made inquiry, and the cattle belonging to the lady were traced. They were rounded up, picked out by their brand marks, and driven back to her.

For a little time in the early days of my campaign, I was quartered in a town, during a pause in the fighting. I offered my service to a Reverend Mother who directed a hospice for the sick and the destitute. The nuns were very poor. Those to whom they gave asylum, many without clothes, lay on bags of chaff covered by threadbare blankets. The rags they had once worn were so filthy they had to be burned. Food and raiment were collected in the town. Clothing and other necessities were given in charity by the few fortunate townsfolk who still had something to bestow.

A nun set out every morning pushing a handcart from door to door, begging bones, cheese rind, cabbage stalks, or some small gift of money. I was very distressed by the plight of these pitiful folk, and I determined to go foraging for them in the thieves' market. I knew well how to drive a hard bargain. There was one poor woman with diseased lungs, whom I knew would die if she were left without warmth and comfort. I said that I would find her a covering that very day.

I disguised myself in my long hooded riding cloak and set out for the market, accompanied by two nuns bearing baskets. The cobbled square was thronged with townsfolk rummaging through the barrows piled with trophies stolen from the fields of war. Nobody asked questions. We took it for granted the things had been pillaged. There was no law to stop the trade.

I had a little money to spend, and I purchased some stale bread, stunted shriveled roots and windfall apples.

When the baskets were full, I said that I wanted to buy clothes for the poor. The nuns were angry. They said that I must save the money for food. Paupers must not be pampered. They could be covered in meal sacks.

I had promised the sick woman a covering and I was going to find one. My gaze roamed around the market and my eye fell on a barrowload of soldiers' gear. I pushed my way through the crowd and began to look over the trophies. There were archers' gauntlets, saddlecloths and bits of broken saddlery, belts and dagger holders heaped in a muddled pile. I did not see any garment that would please a bedridden woman coughing her lungs out.

Then, by chance, I spotted a flash of green and scarlet at the bottom of the pile. I rummaged and heaved, and pulled out a soft wool strip of emerald green crossed and recrossed with red lines. I recognized the plaid used by Scotch mercenaries, and made from precious fleece. It was exactly what was needed for the woman spitting blood.

The swarthy shopman with gold rings in his ears named a large sum. I shook out the woolen square, pointing to a dark-rimmed gash in it, and offered him half the price. The merchant was furious, and appealed to the crowd for justice. He said it was a beautiful and very costly weaving, and that I was trying to cheat him. He had eight children

to feed. He made gestures and the crowd applauded.

I had often heard men haggling in the market and remembered the arguments they used. The shopman shouted bad names at me, and I gave him back words of roguish insult I had learned along the highways. Our voices grew rapid and shrill. The two nuns were aflutter for my audacity. They could only twitter, and pluck at my sleeve to get me away.

I meant to buy the plaid. I draped myself in it, trailing its folds in the mire, and appealed to the crowd. I gave a dramatic imitation of the sick woman's cough. I wished to touch the hearts of the onlookers. Would they not help me? A crowd gathered around us. The merchant gesticulated, crying to Heaven for vindication, swearing that he would have me locked up for trying to beat down his price. The piece was worth three times what he had asked me!

I held up my last remaining coins. Suddenly a well-dressed man pushed forward, took off his plumed hat, flung in a piece of silver, and handed the hat around to the crowd. He called for money in the name of God, to give to the hospice. Coins rained down, and soon he had collected enough to pay the price the merchant had first named. The money slid jingling into the merchant's purse, and I folded the precious wool over my shoulder. The crowd clapped their hands with delight and gave the nuns more coins.

We set off home in triumph. I carried the baskets, and the nuns bore our prize between them as tenderly as a princeling of the blood royal.

A crowd followed us to the hospice, a crowd of beggars afflicted with deformities, terrible ailments and weeping sores. One child dragged a goat and offered milk for the sick woman. We had to drive the crowd from the doors.

The Reverend Mother reviewed our purchases and set the nuns to shred the roots into the iron pot. I was sent into the yard with a brush to scrub and wash the plaid. A trickle of brownish water gushed from the pump, and I went on my knees to scrub away the grime of battle. I slapped and rinsed the woolen piece, and heaved it over the cord. It was very heavy, and it sagged down, dark and wet. Rivulets of muddy water eeled about the paving stones.

Next day I found the plaid sweet and dry, glowing in radiant color. I unraveled wool from the fringe and darned the stab wound with tiny stitches. I held my work at arm's length for the nuns to admire, and the Reverend Mother told me to take it myself to the woman.

I tiptoed into the long, low-ceilinged room where the sick lay. The windows were shuttered, for the air outside was evil-smelling and full of pestilence. "Water, water!" came the cry from many throats, but water was precious and costly. It must be closely rationed.

When my eyes became accustomed to the darkness, I moved between the prostrate bodies, searching for my woman. I called her name, but there was no answer, for when I found her she was quite dead. I pulled the rags over her face and went to fetch help.

At the far corner of the ward, came the wail of a babe, rising and falling like a gull's cry. Under the fogged yellow gleam of lantern light, I saw a body lying with a babe in her arms. She was a mere child herself and pitifully thin. I supported the mother's head on my arms. Tenderly I wrapped the plaid around her and made her son warm and comfortable. She sank back on the floor contented and at peace, with a smile of gratitude, compensation for all time. I blessed her.

Then I went downstairs to help the holy sisters prepare the day's broth.

A calamity of which I will tell wreaked havoc with our camp. A fool put down a powder keg beside our fire, and fed the flames with brushwood. The seams of the barrel were gaping from the drought and a spark fell on it. I remember a crash and roar as of an army beating gongs. I was tossed in the air and fell, with the earth heaving under me. I staggered to my feet, sick and dizzy as if I had been felled by a mailed fist.

Everywhere there was turmoil and distress—smoke, fire, and noise of screaming. Tents spouted plumes of yellow flame. Horses stampeded, men ran like frightened ants. I tried to give orders and direct men to drag gear to safety. I staggered about like a drunkard, getting the worst-burned men to safety. The canvas guttered and flared and tumbled in blackened ruin. Our blankets were alight, the guy ropes, the fodder. There were myriads of small blazes. The red sky rained smoldering fragments.

We worked. We laid the burned men on what canvas remained, and sprinkled their burns with meal. The horses were gone. They had torn away, maddened with pain, their ropes charred through as if chewed by rats.

My ears rang with chiming bells, and violet-colored clouds floated before my eyes. I was deathly sick. Help came to us before I gathered strength to pray for it. Villagers arrived from the hamlet nearby. Those ragged half-starved countryfolk were willing to share their few belongings, though little enough they had to give. They did what they could to be of use. Some dragged milking goats, that they might draw a few drops of milk to sweeten the parched mouths of raving men. Some had skins of water, rags, roots, cages full of pigeons, cheese wrapped in cabbage leaves. They even had faggots to

147

repair the burned-out campfire. A few had spades to flatten the earth. They had feared to find us dead.

We gathered about the fire to cook a meal. So rarely was it safe to kindle a fire, that we would march for days, living on parched corn and cheese cakes, for fear of betraying our presence by smoke.

I had an iron pan in the embers, to cook for my escort, who did not eat with the foot soldiers. They crouched on the scorched earth beside me. Fragments of charred gear hung on stakes behind them, drying out after their sousing with water. I broke pigeon eggs into bubbling hog fat and made a succulent meal. We ate from our hands. Village children gathered about the blaze to brown chunks of bread on pointed sticks. They had been scared by the thunderclap. They had thought the world was ending!

By nightfall some kind of order had been restored. The water troughs were filled by helpers bearing buckets from the pond. The water was green and weedy but a necessity they could ill spare, for the English had poisoned the water wells. The terrified horses were brought back to camp. It was

days before they could be ridden. They lost
flesh, and had to be treated like sick soldiers
who refuse to face danger. Worst of all was
the state of my men. Some deserted under
cover of darkness and were never found.
Others pointed to the yawning black hole,
and said the Devil had made it. God was
angry. The war was lost.

A rick had caught fire and the farmer
claimed damage. My men demanded justice,
but the wretched man who had caused the
accident was nowhere to be found.

I had to pray, reason and implore, scold
and threaten, to learn the whereabouts of the
firebrand's home. I sent riders to search for
him. Two days later they returned with the
poor weak-witted creature in irons. His hair
was singed to the skull, his face seared by
burns, his hands wrapped in rags. He was
cheese-white and starving. He had not been
able to steal, and had drunk only swill from
a pig trough, on his wild race homeward
through the night.

He flung himself down before me and
begged for mercy. The wheel had fallen off
the trolley on which the powder kegs were
shifted. He had shouldered them himself

149

and fallen under the weight! He poured out a rambling story that I knew to be false. My men wanted him strung up to the nearest tree and I feared for his life.

The same day, his father came to me, driving a cart filled with clover hay, butter and bacon and herb cordial. He begged me to accept the provisions as an offering. His son had been a trouble since birth. He was addled like an egg, and unfit for farm work. . . . Please, please, would I take him back? I refused. The culprit was set in the cart, under armed escort, to drive home with papa. That was in itself sufficient punishment to be remembered for a lifetime!

Good came from the misadventure. The rumor spread abroad that our camp had been destroyed by fire, and we had lost everything. The fortunes of war can be changed by such rumors. I thought of the bar of fiery red being battered on the anvil to form a hoop of bright silver, to fit a charger's nimble foot. I prayed that we might be like gold, that fire could not injure. Like gold, might we be made more shining and enduring, of greater worth, to be used for God's glory.

I remember another time, when thunder was my help and stay. I was very much troubled as to what I should do. Pray as I would, I could get no clear guidance. I consulted hardened war veterans, who advised me against my better judgment. My instinct prompted me in one direction, my reason in another. I had to make a decision, because the matter could not be left for even another hour. Were we to attack, or wait until supplies reached us? We might overreach ourselves. Yet by delay we might lose the chance of entering a town of great strategic value.

I lifted myself up to God with one last impassioned prayer, and the answer came to me.

I gave the order to advance. My captain

shook his head and muttered, the soldiers complained. There was very deep resentment, for the men were fatigued and hungry, in no shape for a fresh engagement. I tried to rally them. I told them to fear nothing, but my decision did not win favor.

We rode on, as confident as we could persuade ourselves to be. We met strong opposition and the fighting was hard. I urged my horse soldiers forward in a last charge, and we lost many men. There were dead and wounded all about us. We were hopelessly outnumbered. For an instant my heart failed me and I thought we would have to retreat.

Then a miracle happened, or so it seemed to me. There came the crash of thunder! The English horses were affrighted. Clouds rained silver arrows, the earth shook, lightning quivered and the sky seemed ablaze in yellow flames. It was as if all Heaven came to our aid. The enemy fled in wild disorder, unable to hold formation. My own forces, out of control, bolted after them. Men fell and were trampled on. Riderless horses reared and plunged. There was mad confusion.

We entered the town, deserted because of the storm. Not an arrow struck us. The half-starved inhabitants came out to welcome us. They lit great fires on the cobbles to dry our gear. Our supply wagons arrived full of soaking provender. We spread the blankets to dry, with pulpy bread loaves and wet hay. And the sun burned golden and hot.

I knew in my heart that the enemy would not attack that night. Nuns clustered around us to bind the wounded. Townsfolk offered to fight beside me, bearing perhaps a rusty pike or a meat cleaver. The dead were given Christian burial, the riderless horses were added to our ranks.

I went into the great gray church alone, to give thanks for God's thunder.

n the time since I became a soldier, used now to privation, toil, and all the weariness of battle, never did I grow accustomed to the weight of armor. My charger flung me forth and back as if I were on cradle rockers, and sent warm sweat trickling down inside the stiff bark that held me, bruised and battered me as if by blows.

I had brave men to care for, shared their danger and their pain. I prayed for them, listened to their sad complaint and dressed their wounds. They had bellyache and saddle sores, swelled feet, and blistered hands. Often the strongest would swoon at the sight of gushing blood. Food was bad, water foul. We were short of dressings.

I spent long hours beside the dying, bathing their blanched faces, as they whispered and groaned. They called for their mothers like children and blasphemed in their pain. Men feigned illness to escape work, or escaped to join the enemy. Carts shed their iron wheel rims and foundered in the mire. Our precious stores were spoiled by rain.

It was my custom, my great delight, to make confession frequently, for no man may keep his conscience too clean.

This happened in a big monastery that I visited whilst on campaign. When I had confessed, the Reverend Father took me into his own cell, that he might question me further. The cell was of cold stone, with a keyhole window high in the wall. Through it shone shafts of gold sunlight. There was a rack filled with parchment scrolls. On a scribe's desk, laid out with brushes and paintpots, lay a half-finished missal.

I admired the vermilion letterings, intertwined with braids of rainbow color, gay birds and beasts. There were great gouts of beaten gold, dull or adazzle as they caught the light. I wished that I had the learning to read the text.

I sat on a chair facing the Reverend

Father, with two monks standing like sentinels behind me. On the wall before me hung a cross. I looked up at the pitiful figure nailed upon it, and sought to calm my pounding heart by thinking of Him.

"My daughter, you have made clean confession." The Father was a kindly-faced man, gaunt, white-haired, and stooping with age. "But I am greatly disturbed by what is being said about you. I do not as yet see in you the sin of pride, but I would know more. What religious instruction have you had?"

"One of the friars who preaches at the wayside cross at Domremy has instructed me in the holy Faith. My mother and our own dear priest," I answered boldly. "Our priest said that my contrition was so deep that he would have liked to send me to a sisterhood, for I had the calling to become a nun. My parents refused, and I gave myself over to obey their will."

"This is not my belief," answered the holy man. "I think you defied the wish of your parents, in riding with soldiers and leaving home. What do you know of Saint Catherine?"

156

"She is a virgin martyr invoked by many on the bed of death." I looked into his deep sunken eyes, of rain-washed gray. He was watching me closely. "My mother taught me about her. She came to me in a crown of fretted gold like a church tower, and a green cloak with gems set in the border, bright and sparkling. I have embraced her and I know that she is real."

My answer did not please him. He shook his head over my delight at her jewels.

I went on telling him of my life. I said that I could do most things on a farm—plow, reap, and deliver a lamb. I had chosen to wear a youth's raiment out of modesty, that I might appear as a man amongst men. I had not become a soldier out of any love for notoriety. My lot was not to be envied. I was in constant danger and my labors never ceased. The meanest lout of a turnip-head foot soldier had far less to bear! The Mission that the great God had given me had not brought me ease.

He questioned me about Saint Michael.

"He wore armor as we do," I said. "He was a full gracious, kind, sweet-tempered, good man, with a shining face. He was

delicately nurtured, and of the finest be-
havior and bearing. He had no wings. I felt
warmed and comforted, befriended, and
very pleased to be of use to him. I will go
on so long as he needs me. I shall not cease
until I have driven the English out of
France!"

The Reverend Father shook his head.
"You have heard tales of the Lady Margaret,
and seen the angel in the church window.
You have heard travelers' tales and have a
lively liking for adventure, my daughter.
You are a brave girl, but unwise. How do
you know that what you *think* you see, is the
person you believe you see?"

This made me very angry. How did I
know?

"I know, because I know, Reverend
Father," I said, trying to keep my voice from
trembling. "How do I know my pigeons?
Of course I know them, each one of them.
I call them by name as they whicker down
like an army to peck and jostle, and preen
and coo. I know them as I know my friends.
I know them by their little faces!"

The monks made a sound in their throats,
and the Father hid a smile with his hand.

158

He stared full at me, with such intensity that I felt discomfited, but I held my ground. How did I know my Saints, indeed? I said to myself. I knew them by their perfume, their voices, their counsel. Had Saint Catherine not stood by my couch and shaken me awake, told me to take horse, for a surprise attack had been planned by the enemy? I had buckled on my armor, aroused my sleepy page, and gone clattering through the town in the early hours, riding toward the river. I aroused the sentries, told them to man the bridge and gather every man that could bear arms. An army was approaching over the water, floating on boats bolted together with bracing irons. We were able to meet them before they had hooked one ladder to the walls. Our archers sent arrows whirling down, and drove them back in confusion. I knew! I knew my Saints were true.

The Father bowed his head in prayer. When he looked at me again, the thundercloud had vanished from his face.

"You are right, my daughter. I doubted and was torn in twain by what you told me. I feared that the Devil had ensnared you, but God has told me that you are right.

Go in peace. My monks shall pray for you."

"Amen. May God keep me forever in His Grace, and save the soul of every French soldier in battle," I said fervently, and I crossed myself.

I rose up, bowed courteously, and the interrogation ended. We walked together down the dim stone corridor, brightened by little squares of yellow sunshine, like the gold on the parchment. My long spurs clicked, my heart thudded like hooves on turf, and the sandaled feet of the two monks behind us clapped like hands.

One monk turned the thick key, a handspan long. The other swung open the ironbound oaken door, that bayed like a hound on its hinges. I offered grease, from a small jar I carried, to set it at peace. I wished that I might stitch the monk's unraveled hem, for I was good at sewing. Could I not do some small service? Prepare the roots for broth? I hesitated and bit my fingers. The words refused to form. I was shy in the presence of those stern monks, unaccustomed as they were to a woman's presence.

I went out on the whitened steps. The sky made a tent of blue, arching above the grim building dedicated to mortification and prayer. The Reverend Father stood in the doorway smiling, and answered my heart's cry.

"You are the ward of Michael the Archangel, Mademoiselle Jeanne. There will never be need for you to fear!"

His smile fell upon me like a caress. The plated door, cumbersome as a knight's armor, clanged behind me. I was alone in the garden save for the brothers tending the flower beds, and the darting birds. My knights were impatiently awaiting my return in the road outside. My heart was filled with a burning joy to be alive.

God's soldier!

I was in a small market town as it grew dusk. My horse fell lame, so that I would not be able to ride him back to camp. I said that I would find myself quarters for the night. My bodyguard of knights assured me they would fetch me another mount.

We had a heated argument. I wanted to ride down a narrow cobbled lane that twisted away from the main square. The alley was known as Snatch-Purse Lane. I wore a youth's ill-fitting raiment and looked like a young man. I said that I would ride alone down the evil-looking street, to seek a farrier who would shoe my horse. My knights, angry and suspicious, said they would come to seek me if I did not speedily return.

It was a filthy lane with a gutter down the middle full of oily black water, evil-smelling and choked with decaying refuse. The tumbling houses leaned crazily forward, like drunken men trying to embrace. The walls shut out the clean air. The blistered plaster looked like running sores. The thatch was black and moldered. It had fallen between rafters which shone in bare bones.

Half-naked children waded out of the drain to swarm around me and snatch at my saddlecloth with birdlike claws. Some held shriveled babes, with lolling heads and sunken eye sockets leaden-blue.

"Have you come for the *dog*, soldier-boy?" they whimpered. "Marie, our queen, was chased by a dog. It belongs to a rich lady. We know she will find it. She will have us put in the jail."

"I have come to find a man who will attend to my horse," I said. He was slithering and pawing on the slimy cobbles. Children were all about him, tumbling under his belly.

I wanted to turn back before I was set on by thieves, dragged down and stabbed. The

bends in the lane hid my knights from view. I was quite alone. I regretted ever having come to such a place. Wicked bloated faces leered out at me from behind broken shutters. Barking dogs were snapping at my horse's heels.

"We will take you to Marie." said one of the older children. "She tried to grab a purse from a lady but it was linked to her bracelet. She let her dog go, and Marie caught it, but it will bring us trouble. Marie can cure horses. She will help you, if you will help us!"

"Take the dog!" they all cried. We had reached a house with a timber yard adjoining. The children gave three owl hoots, and a small head looked out of a top window. "Come down, Marie, there is a fine young soldier who will take back the dog," sang out an older boy softly, through cupped hands.

I looked up to see a thin little girl straddle the windowsill, lean head down to grasp a leaden gutter pipe, and then come slithering to the ground. The children flung themselves on the cobbles before her and hailed her as queen. She was an ugly little girl, with tousled yellow hair, and thin naked limbs showing through the rents in her rags. She was very frightened and looked anxiously up the lane toward the town.

"Listen to me, Master Soldier," she said. "You must go *at once,* or you will be killed for your boots and spurs! My subjects are angry because I did not pick a purse full of silver. I am in danger too. Take back the dog I filched, and I will cure your horse. I have strange powers of healing.

"Take the dog away before we have worse fortune! Take the dog, please, sire. It is the *dog* that is ruining us!" The children were bleating like hurt sheep. I was hemmed in on every side, and near to fainting in the press.

I heard a growl. A dog was being bundled out of the timber yard. The poor creature was tied around with rags and cord to hide his form. My stirrup leather was unhooked and thrust through the spiked collar. The leash was knotted to my belt.

Marie had taken charge of my horse, like a practiced groom, and led him away. I was forced forward by a heaving swarm of men and women who had joined us, excited by the noise. I had no strength to resist. A cloth was flung over my head so that I could not see where I was going.

"Take the dog back to its owner, or we will crack Marie's head like an egg, for starving us," said a rough voice. The dog sprang forward, and I was kept moving. I walked for a long time. Then suddenly the rag was snatched away, and the sound of running feet grew fainter. I found myself dazed and alone in the dark town, with a fierce dog tied to my belt.

I went up the steps of a house and knocked. After a long wait, a woman appeared, swathed in a blanket, having been aroused from sleep. She tried to shut the door in my face, but I stuck in my boot. I asked if I might spend the night in some attic, as I was lost. I had found a stray dog that might be valuable, but it was too late to seek the owner. The woman threatened me and said she would do no such thing. Two children appeared behind her. The dog began to bark. Windows opened in the neighboring houses. Men and women looked out and told me to take the dog away and let them sleep.

The children were on their knees examining the dog collar. One unhooked a lantern from the hall and they examined him closely. They said they knew him for certain. He was Carlo, the beloved Carlo, from the great house. "Carlo! Carlo!" they cried and the dog wagged his tail.

"I cannot have you in the house, but in the morning my children shall lead you to Carlo's mistress," said the lady, and she shut the door in my face.

I was left alone on the doorstep in the dark. I coiled myself up on the steps to wait for daylight. Carlo was tied so securely to my belt that I could not free him. He howled and a window opened. A bucket of water was emptied on my head, and this revived me.

At the first light of dawn, I set out to search for my knights. I was in the more prosperous part of the town, in a street lined with shops. Boys were coming out to unlock shutters and sweep the steps. One of them cut Carlo free from my belt, and the dog ran beside me and found a bone.

A man appeared, driving a cow. I had enough money to buy a cup of milk. He said that it was market day, and if I waited in the square, Carlo's mistress would surely be at the market.

I found my way to the square, buckled Carlo to a paling and sat on the curb to wait for the stalls to open. Carts drove in from the country, laden with pigs and geese. The farmers penned their beasts and spread their wares upon the cobbles.

I decided to try to find my horse. Snatch-Purse Lane was alive with activity. Screaming children were busy poking in the gutter for what they could find, hurling dirt and fighting. I heard horse hooves coming toward me, clipper-clop. It was my horse, with a small rider perched astride. The children fell back and stood to attention, arms raised in a salute.

I stared hard. It was Marie, and yet not Marie, but a boy with tangled flaxen hair.

"Marie, our queen, our queen, bring us back silver and bread!" sang the children with one voice. I caught the bridle rein of my horse, and the young rider dismounted and made a low bow.

"Good-day to you, Monsieur Soldier," said Marie with a merry grin. "I must tell you that I am a boy. I wear woman's rags to work the market and for taking a babe out begging. Your horse has been shod and will be sound within three days, for I have healing fingers. I will keep your things for payment. Your clippers and spare cloak."

I stooped to examine the hoof. Quick as a bird, Marie hopped up astride again and kicked my horse into a gallop. I had to jump over the gutter, and I slipped and fell, to the joy of the children.

I hurried back to the market and found a lovely lady clad in costly raiment, smothering Carlo's moist snout with kisses.

Marie was beside her, holding my horse.

"It was *I* who saved your dog from the thieves of Snatch-Purse Lane," boasted Marie. "I am a page boy to the soldier here. I chased the girl who tried to grab your purse. I chased her and beat her blue, and went into the thieves' den, and fought every one of them, and got your dog, before they put him in the cooking pot. I ran out with him, and spent the night hiding, for I knew they would kill me."

"You are a very brave, good boy. I wish we had more like you to save France," said the lady, counting out coins from the purse that swung from her bracelet. She laid her head on Carlo's hairy one, and called him sweet names.

When she had unbuckled the strap from the rails, she gave a cry, for her bag had been cut from her wrist. Marie had vanished into the crowd. My saddlebags were empty. Later, I found some of my things displayed on a market stall, and bought them back.

My knights found me. They had had a terrible fight with the crowd of thieves, and had ransacked the town in search of me. The lady took us to her home, and gave us food and water. When we were rested, we set out again, meaning to ride back to camp. I would not leave the town without going again down Snatch-Purse Lane in search of Marie, accompanied by my men.

When I struck the door with my sword, Marie stuck his head out of the upper window.

"I will take you as a page, if you will give back the purse," I called up to him.

"No I thank you, soldier-boy," Marie shouted down. "I am rich and my luck has changed. I will make a matchless thief in your riding cloak, cut to fit. I would rather be queen of Snatch-Purse Lane." He tossed down the velvet purse, quite empty, and closed the window.

y men had won a hard fought battle and we entered the town in triumph. A banquet had been arranged in my honor. I, with a few of my trusted knights, was invited to the home of a wealthy citizen, to be given wine and welcome. I was greatly touched by the kindness of the burghers, who had obtained food at high cost, because of its scarcity. Times were lean. Even the great ladies were hollow-cheeked from hunger. On the dais of the dining hall sat the host and his lady, at the center of the fine carven table spread with dishes. I sat at my host's right hand: Counselors, lawyers, guildsmen, other prominent citizens, and my knights attendant took the remaining places.

It was a noble hall and I stared, with eyes full of wonderment, at its glory. The floor was spread with rugs like jeweled windows for color, soft and mossy as an April lawn. The furniture was scrolled and massive, padded with bolsters of brocade. The wood shone like a ripe chestnut. On the walls hung paintings of lords and ladies of a bygone age, framed in golden rims. The tall windows, filled with diamond glass, were rich with crests and fabulous beasts wrought in enamel and golden leaf. The banquet board was illumined by pure white wax candles held in twisted columns of silver. They shed little crescents of brightness on the shining platters.

I felt very ill at ease. Weariness pressed down on me and I feared lest I fall asleep in the presence of this awesome assemblage.

I had eaten trout wet with grassy sauce, and pigeon pie with quarters of hard-cooked eggs. Then came a rich pastry, and I knew the moment when I would be expected to speak was near. I slipped my uneaten pastry to the little warm dog who coiled at my feet.

The hostess stood up and clapped her hands. I could see by her milk-white fingers that she was not used to work. She must despise me from the bottom of her heart. The clamor of conversation trailed into silence. Leaning over me, with mock politeness the lady asked me to tell of my victory.

The guests banged down their goblets and I felt their eyes upon me. I took a sip of wine and by pressing the rim of the table pulled myself up. I shook like a stem of corn left by the reapers. I thought the aldermen looked like grass-bloated sheep, unclipped and heavy. The sparks from their bright chains hurt my eyes.

"My lords, ladies, good men and staunch, all those assembled," I mumbled with great effort. "You have done us much honor, but God calls us to go on fighting, to be like hounds in chase—" My words were drowned by furious barking of the dog under the table.

A serving maid came and whispered to my hostess.

"A crowd of poor folk would see the Maid," said my hostess, bowing her tall steeple hat toward me. "They are rough and uncontrolled. I think we should set the dogs on them and drive them away before they have done damage. Send Antoine to bar the shutters."

"I will speak to them," I said. Before my knights could stop me, I ran from the room, holding the skirts of the banquet robe that greatly restricted my movements.

I was astraddle the window ledge in the corridor before the old servingman and maids could bar the shutters. They latched the window behind me and cut off my retreat. I was outside on the stone ledge, a lance length above the crowd. I faced a multitude of men and women, dirty and half-starved, more like bones held together in peeled leather than live human creatures. They had lifted the gate of the yard from its hinges and poured in, like ants from a stricken nest.

I spoke to them, when I could make myself heard. I said that God would help them. They must go to the cathedral and pray for deliverance. They held up to me their stumps, their deformed limbs, and little wizened babes with crooky frog legs. They tore off their rags, waved their crutches, and suddenly turned in despair and violence upon each other. There was great uproar.

Soldiers thrust their way in from the street, and beat the crowd back with the butt ends of pikes. The people clasped me by the feet and tried to drag me down. My robe was torn.

The window opened behind me and I was forcibly dragged inside the house by the servants. I was powerless to prevent the hungry watchdogs being let loose to clear the yard. The servants barred the gateway with an old carriage, and began to sweep up the horrible mess that remained. There were torn flowers, broken branches, bits of rag, and an abandoned wailing child.

With the child in my arms, I entered the dining hall. The party were now dancing. They stopped to stare at me. I pushed my way toward the hostess, and dropped on one knee.

"My lady," I said, "my knights will attend me and bear this lost child to the sisterhood. I crave a boon. I would have your servants collect the fragments of the banquet, that we may distribute the food amongst the hungry."

I had my way. I left the child in the care of the holy nuns, with money I begged for her care. My knights had to support me back to the great house, where I was to stay the night.

When I was at last alone, looking down at the wide bed, cool and inviting, I was too dazed to disrobe. They hammered on the door, offering help. I refused. I flung myself down fully clad and stretched out weary and spent.

When I had rested my aching limbs and all the house was still, I roused myself and unlaced the robe that had been provided for the banquet. It was past repair. I slid my body between the soft, lavender-scented sheets laid over ticking filled with feathers plucked from the breasts of geese. I sighed happily, for I had never known such comfort. Certainly not in my home, nor in the ruined barns where I had spent nights on musty straw, with rats gnawing my boots to taste the grease. I felt ashamed for the feast that had been prepared to please me, when the poor in the streets were dying of hunger. A small lamp hung by the Crucifix on the wall. I could see the tapestry above the fireplace, dim, mysterious in the half-darkness. I had seen it by daylight, as I robed myself for the banquet, and much admired the weaving.

As I lay, my head swirling in the warm sweetness, I seemed to split in two. A part of me became a different person, joining in the tapestry hunt. The grass was of brightest emerald, with ferns and bells and little bright stars of blossom worked in wool as real as life. I was seated sideways on a cream-white palfrey.

My horse was playful. He minced and pranced, tossed his body sideways, plunged, bickered, caricolled and gamboled. I played his gentle mouth delicately with a long loose rein, perfectly at my ease. I rode among stems of stiff poplars—trotting, striding, and at a flowing gallop. My knights followed, bearing hooded hawks on their gauntlets. They unfettered the jesses and set the hawks free to soar in the blue. There was a twisty stream, worked in gray and blue stitchery. The water began to flow as I watched, and I saw leaping fish. The hunt came up to join me. Knights and ladies were riding at furious pace. The huntsman blew his horn and the hounds gathered.

They were not like any hound I had ever seen in flesh or vision. They had human faces. They were a pack in cry, with lolling tongues and sharp shiny teeth, cruel, crooked, leering devilish faces. They had the look of the crowd that tore at me, men turned animal by war, thirsting to gnash flesh and lap blood. I saw a little dappled fawn ahead, a gentle creature full of leap and frolic. The hounds bayed with heart-rending dolorous tones as they bore down upon it, their eyes glowing.

The joy died out of me. I no longer took delight in my scarlet saddle and lovely steed. The wild things of the woods, stoats and martens, badgers and hares, were losing their life. They were turning to tapestry. The little rust-red fox, with pricked black-rimmed ears, had frozen with lifted paw. The rabbit, belly to earth, ears laid back, was motionless ahead of him.

I opened my eyes. Daylight was streaming through the slatted shutters. There was the tapestry, stiff and stirring faintly in the draft. It was naught but strands of weft running across and across, and warp threads down and adown. I looked up to Jesus, forlorn in His pain. I told Him of my ride in the flowery dells, the tossing branches of the green wood.

I leaped out of my curtained bed. I knew that I must see the young child the crowd had abandoned—the fawn the hounds were chasing. My boots were cleaned and ready, my youth's raiment brushed and repaired. I laced my hose and girth myself. I reached the servant's quarters and said that I must visit the sisterhood at once.

Two timid maids went with me, with the house dogs on leash.

The sacristan came to the door of the convent.

Ten other children had been abandoned on the doorstep in the night. The Reverend Mother was trying to wash them at that very moment. Could I perchance beg for them more money and food?

O Michael, Michael, Captain of the Angel Host, God's leader, it was for your sweet sake I left my home and entered battle. I chose sword and buckler, war-horse and spurs. For you I ordered armies, I broke the siege of war, I tumbled towers. For you I bled, I charged forward, I triumphed and prevailed, I fell, I entered the flames.

GOD'S PLAN

nly fragments of memory come to me from the days after I was made captive by the English.

You will read in the history books how I became the prisoner of the Earl of Warwick. The Earl believed himself superior to all other men. He would have liked to see the English standard placed on every tower throughout the world.

God gave me words to speak to him, and he was never able to break my spirit, by argument or threat.

I remember the round tower in Rouen, where I lay, chained by the leg to a plank bed. I had eaten poisoned carp and was in a fever. The bread was mildewed, the water foul and I had great pain. I lay, covered only by a filthy blanket.

Some of the guards were gross and brutal. They insulted and abused me. One guard told me that my hair had grown too long for a soldier. He grabbed hold of it and tried to saw it with his knife.

The bolts jarred and jangled as my jailer made the door fast. He pocketed the key and sat down again on his little stool.

I fell back on my plank bed, scarcely feeling the throb in my temples, the pain from my shackled leg, that had broken out in open ulcers. I was in extreme bliss. There was a rush of Holy Spirit descending on me. I felt enveloped in its warm and golden brightness. Words sprang to my lips and rang out as though an angel prompted them.

"My jailer, I am right. I am *right*. I did see the Angel. The Saints come to me. God sent me. He did. He *did*."

"We have heard quite enough from you, Devil's carrion," said the jailer.

He came over to me and struck me over the mouth. The guards tore away my raiment, left me half naked to endure the cold. They kept me awake by their gaming, swearing and drinking. I had no peace nor privacy.

I now know that I was burned by the

powers I was sent to destroy. As the false-hoods against me increased, so did the comfort of the Saints, that I might bear my suffering bravely.

The Blessed Mary came to me, when all the world was silent. Even the swinish English guards had stopped their dicing and fallen asleep.

Thin swords of silver moonlight stabbed through the slit window above my head. Otherwise the tower was in darkness, for my guards had covered the lantern that they might sleep the sounder. A bout of shivering shook my body. I bit my hand to keep from moaning, lest my guards strike me for waking them.

Suddenly I knew there was someone beside me. In the gray, dappled dimness at my feet I could see the outline of a woman. She was wrapped from head to heel in blue-gray clinging folds that melted and formed again. I watched her take shape, and I knew, in my heart, that my ghostly visitor came from God. She pulled aside the cheeks of her hood, and a shaft of silver illumined her face. I saw a young woman in the pride of youth, but her eyes were in shadow. She was speaking. I clenched my teeth to stop their chatter, that I might hear her soft low voice.

"Daughter Jeanne," she said, "I am Mary, the Mother of your Lord."

A perfume as of warm, sweet brier came to my nostrils, and I beheld light, primrose pale at first, but brightening, until every cranny of my grim prison was illumined. I could see the cobwebs hanging like old gray shawls from the rafters in the peaked roof. I could count the clumsy, knobbled nail-heads in the iron-barred door. Every pebble and flint was brightened by the light.

I found comfort in the delicate and tender face of my Lady. I closed my eyes and fell into a doze.

The walls of my prison melted and I was outside, falling, falling. I opened my eyes, to find myself lying in the scented grass of the water meadow by my home. There was the river, coiling long gray-green tresses. The stream was dappled by cloud patterns, patches of blue sky, and licked by flames of golden sunlight. I saw the familiar willows, the foam-tufted meadowsweet, yellow iris clumps and sceptered bullrushes. All about me were the flowers I loved, wild pea and thyme, pimpernel and blue bird's eye. Bright grass shook its dust over me, as I lay stretched out, sun-soaked and at ease.

I rested. My pain was gone.

I wakened to find myself in prison. I heard the iron bar jarring in its metal hoop as the door opened and the guard was changed. A man brought me a jug of water and a round of black bread. After the usual blasphemy and insult, the shackle was knocked from my infected leg and I was unchained.

I was so weak that I had to be dragged down the stone stairway, one leg trailing useless like the broken leg of a doll. I was given a mouthful of fresh air to prepare me for my interrogation. I had to cling to the jailer for fear of fainting.

When I was taken to the courtroom I scarce heeded my captors. I heard Mary's voice to prompt me in my answers. She told me, as I faced my examiners, that I must bear unjust trial, and lies, as did Jesus, her Son.

My trial was unworthy to be called a trial. It was an interrogation under threat. There was bribery and corruption. The treacherous Bishop Cauchon was paid by the English to hound me to death. Cauchon took lessons from a lawyer who showed him how to build his case to discredit me both as a leader and as a woman. There were promoters of lies in the monasteries and even in the court itself, paid to discredit me. I wore fine raiment to capture the admiration of men. I had not only disgraced my womanhood by wearing man's attire, I had besmirched the fair honor of France by my absurd claim. I was given no chance to obtain counsel. Many of my answers were falsified or omitted altogether.

The Bishop of Beauvais directed against me most horrible malice, knowing that God had given me certain gifts that he much envied. He never for one moment suspected me of being a witch.

After my capture I found that the English *did* really think me a demon, so cleverly had the rumors been spread. They came to question me, expecting to find the Archfiend in person. It had become an accepted fact that I invoked devils, that I *was* a devil, a witch, a black sorceress.

I said the lies told against me came from Satan. I was a countrywoman and content with my condition. I had been offered marriage. I would have been a wife and reared children like others of our station and kind.

God changed my destiny. He used me like a chessman on the board. He sent me to drive out the invader.

I vowed to remain chaste and never lowered my dignity with the soldiers. Only if I held myself aloof could I with safety carry God within my heart.

They tried to prove me wrong. The Duke of Normandy had conquered England and they felt it was right that his sons should inherit the French throne.

The lie that I was a witch was brewed in England as a suitable means of ending my campaign. It was the invention of a councillor in the Court of Henry VI.

The story that I was a witch was a clever piece of deception. I now know every step of the plot. It sent me to God's highest Heaven in the shortest possible time! My enemies did me the greatest *good*, although the way they chose was uncomfortable and not to be imposed on those too weak to bear so harsh a cross.

I was dragged from the cart and lifted onto the pile of faggots. A chain was locked around my waist. I wore a coarse, hempen robe and the heretic's mitre of parchment was stuck upon my head, but I was so much numbed by fear I scarce knew what was happening.

For those who feel for my pain, I will say

that my torment lasted but one brief instant. I heard my body cry, but I was outside it, above it in the swirling smoke, attached only by a shining cord of silver. Michael came for me, and sliced me free with his sword, and carried me high above the crowd of noisy men and soldiers, screaming, moaning, beating their breasts and in tears. I caught one last glimpse of the poor, blackened thing in the flames, like banners, licking their dragon tongues about the stake. Then I fell asleep in Michael's arms.

My death caused a wave of terrible despair to sweep through France. I was beloved of the countryfolk, who never believed that I was evil. It was a lie invented by the Devil himself. Had I denied having been sent by God to deliver France, my life would have been spared. This I refused to do, because I never doubted. I was sure the King of Heaven had sent me, and I was able to endure, even death itself.

When I had left earth, I met the man who had built the pyre on which I was burned. He was a brutish and ignorant yokel, but he asked me to pardon him, for he had had no choice but to do as he was told. He had been a servant in the household of the mayor. He was not the man usually employed for the work of building a pyre. That is why his name is not recorded in the town's official records. He drew faggots from a cart and laid them in a pattern according to ancient custom. He built the pyre carefully, using green sticks that I might linger in my torment. When he had done, he was proud of his job, and went home and enjoyed a hearty meal. He really liked the idea of seeing a witch burned. He was not in the least upset in his stomach and had a good night. He thought that I was a witch and deserved burning. He was given a handsome reward for his pains.

I helped Charles find his crown. I rode beside him through cheering crowds. I fought and fell, and he deserted me. After my capture he left me forgotten and abandoned. He met me again after his death, and Pierre Cauchon too, the Bishop who killed me, and I interceded that he might escape hell, but not purgatory. He was punished for what he had done. He saw me in the glory that God gave me, and I held *him* to trial in the Court on High, and he was *my* prisoner, as I had been his.

I have visited the market place where I was burned and have knelt on the paving stones above the old cobbles. Crowds pass, women pushing babies in wheel carts, noisy machines bellowing like angry oxen, men in unfamiliar raiment. A stray dog saw me, as I prayed for France. He fled in terror, howling, with his tail between his legs.

France has changed. Even the art of killing has changed. The castles are ruined and gone. The vineyard is a cornfield. The river runs between stiff banks, but I can see into the earth—the streams where once we cleansed our broken bodies and drank like hunted beasts, the rutted cart tracks where our wagons foundered, the tented fields. It is there, the ancient land, the scarred earth, for those who have the vision, deep, deep beneath the scarlet bricks and tall chimneys, the towns and factories, and metal runways, the winding ribbons of hard blue shiny roads.

I know now, that God can use defeat to further His purpose, as surely as victory, and that my life and my death were part of His plan.

Jeanne d'Arc was born at Domremy on the Meuse River in 1412, during the Hundred Years War between France and England.

Obedient to the call of Saint Michael, Jeanne rallied French forces and led them against the English and their Burgundian allies. She freed Orléans and made possible the crowning at Rheims of the Dauphin, King Charles VII of France.

Captured by the Burgundians in the spring of 1430, Jeanne d'Arc was sold to the English and turned over to a French ecclesiastical court. Accused of heresy and tried as a witch, she was convicted. A secular court condemned her to death and in 1431 she was burned at the stake in the marketplace at Rouen.

Twenty-five years after her death, ecclesiastical authority annulled her sentence.

Maid of Lorraine, standard-bearer of France, Jeanne d'Arc was declared a Saint in 1920.